IMAGINATION CHECKERS

Cricket & Kyle—Book 1

ENDORSEMENTS

This heartwarming story shows us how a simple game combined with friendship and imagination can bring joy to even the toughest situation.
—Stephanie Sharp, elementary school media specialist

Thoughtfully written. I love how each character is so carefully explored. You can tell they were written with care. I can't wait to read this to my students. My daughter and I thoroughly enjoyed reading this together.
—Debbie Christ, M.Ed ESE School Specialist

I've so enjoyed reading about Cricket and Kyle with my students. Imagination Checkers is full of everything young readers crave, all in vivid word pictures. So glad for a new series we can't wait to read. Especially looking forward to seeing the illustrations.
—Melody R., tutor

I loved it and can't wait to find out what happens in the next adventure!
—Julia S., kid reader

Christy Adams is an imaganitive storyteller, and her book is a lively action-packed tale that will keep young readers engaged. The themes of family bonds, deep friendships, the power of laughter and of prayer, are set amid a young child's bout with a serious life threatening disease.
—Rose Knox, teacher and author

IMAGINATION CHECKERS

Cricket & Kyle—Book 1

CHRISTY BASS ADAMS

ILLUSTRATED BY

LISA ISADORA THOMPSON

Katelynn,
Enjoy ever
moment of fun
and adventure!

COPYRIGHT NOTICE

Imagination Checkers—Cricket & Kyle Book 1

Cover and Interior Design: Lisa Isadora Thompson, Derinda Babcock, Deb Haggerty

Editor(s): Yvonne MacKay, Deb Haggerty

Author Represented By:

PUBLISHED BY: Elk Lake Publishing, Inc., 35 Dogwood Drive, Plymouth, MA 02360, 2022

Library Cataloging Data

Names: Adams, Christy Bass (Christy Bass Adams)

Imagination Checkers—Cricket & Kyle Book 1 / Christy Bass Adams

146 p. 23cm × 15cm (9in × 6 in.)

ISBN-13: 978-1-64949-736-9 (paperback) | 978-1-64949-737-6 (trade hardcover) | 978-1-64949-738-3 (trade paperback) | 978-1-64949-739-0 (e-book)

Key Words: Middle-grade; children's cancer; friendships; intergenerational relationships; grandparents; imagination; games

Library of Congress Control Number: 2022946686 Fiction

DEDICATION

To the dream that sat on the shelf too long ...
it's time to LIVE!

TABLE OF CONTENTS

ACKNOWLEDGMENTS

AUTHOR

Thank you, Mom and Dad, for all the silliness growing up. For wordplays, games, and tardy notes written in limerick or haiku. Science experiments, cloud gazing, and forcing us to play outside. So much of my imagination and creativity is a direct result of being raised by clowns (I mean that in the best, most loving way possible).

Carter and Daniel, you two keep me and Dada silly. I'm grateful God chose you to be our sons.

Vicki, you won't let me settle. Thank you for pushing me to chase my dreams.

Thank you, Julia and Madison, for being my first kid readers when this journey started so many years ago. Knowing you loved the story gave me the courage to keep moving forward, especially when I was scared.

Yvonne Mackay, my amazing editor, you made this process a pure delight. Your thoughtful, humorous sidebars made me feel like I was talking with an old friend. The way you became intimately acquainted with my characters warmed my heart. Thank you for your coaching, editing, and friendship.

Deb and Cristel, thank you for believing in the project and opening the door to publication.

Lisa Thompson, I can't even begin to express how awesome I felt seeing the scenes I wrote come to life in pictures. Thank you for jumping in with both feet and making this book a reality. I'm grateful for you.

And thank you to my tribe of friends and readers. I feel so loved and encouraged by you. Thank you for the regular encouragement and reminders that help me stay focused. I could not do any of this without you.

And thank you, God, for this wonderful gift of words. I am truly grateful.

ILLUSTRATOR

I would like to express my gratitude to Christy for inviting me on this adventure with Cricket and Kyle. I so appreciate your trust in me and the creative freedom to bring these characters to life on paper.

This project would not have been possible without the love and support of my husband and children who supplied me with honest, constructive feedback, and maybe more importantly, continuous snacks and hot cups of tea during all of those months and late night hours in the studio.

Finally, my parents, who were always being my cheerleaders. I know my dad would be proud.

—1—
SNAKE CHARMING

"Put that snake down!" Grammy yelled. "You're gonna get yourself killed one of these days!"

I straightened my headdress and went back to sitting cross-legged while Poppy yelled over his shoulder, "It's just a rat snake, Lois. Give it a rest, will you?"

Poppy put the snake into Grammy's old breadbasket and sat across from me with his legs crisscrossed. Snake charming took a lot of patience and focus. Poppy rocked from side to side as he "charm-fully" played my recorder. He played *London Bridge*, *Old McDonald*, *Twinkle, Twinkle*, and *Rock-a-Bye Baby* while we watched the basket.

That stubborn snake didn't even twitch or blink his eyes. He was by far the laziest snake I'd ever been around. What good was snake charming if the dumb ole snake couldn't be charmed? You'd think a snake that's been captured would try to escape, but not this one.

"Oh, well, Cricketbug. We gave it a fair shot. We've tried playing every song we can think of. I've held him. You've held him. We tried dancing with him, staring into his eyes, and even tempting him with a fat, juicy mouse Grammy caught in her glue trap, but that snake refuses to be charmed. Let's take Grammy back her breadbasket."

Poppy grabbed the basket and got a head start while I packed up the checkerboard. When I tried to catch up to him, the lid of the basket lifted a little. Maybe I was imagining things. As Poppy walked up the steps, I saw the lid lift again. "Poppy, don't take the basket inside, yet." I ran to catch up with him, but he didn't hear me.

As I got to the bottom step, I heard Poppy say from inside the house, "Lois, I wouldn't worry about that dumb, old snake in your breadbasket. Shake him out in your flowerbed. He's either stunned or dead, so either way you've got nothing to worry about."

"Don't you leave that snake in my house!" Grammy yelled from the back room. Poppy pretended he didn't hear her and left the basket on the edge of the counter, kind of giggling as he walked away.

When he opened the screen door to the porch, I whispered, "Poppy, that snake is alive." We turned just in time to see the lid of the basket lift up and the snake slide down the outside. "We better get out of here, Poppy! Grammy's going to be so mad."

As we made our way around the side of the house all we heard was, WHAM! SPLATT! WHACK!

"Todd! I'm gonna get you for this!"

IMAGINATION CHECKERS

BAAM! SMACK!
"One of these days, old man!"
All we could do was giggle.

—2—
NO MORE DANCING

The next day, I zoomed through the back door. Grammy threw her arms up in the air and yelled, "Well, I'll be!"

I rounded the corner and grabbed my old-timey dancing dress, my flea-market, white high-heeled flip-flops, and my huge, old-lady hat with a bright pink flower. Dancing day was the best.

Poppy always grabbed my hand, spun me in a circle, asked who I was and what I had done with his little Cricketbug. I'd smile and say, "I'm your little Cricketbug, Poppy!"

He'd whistle and say, "Well, I do declare, I believe you are my little Cricketbug! Would you care to have this dance?"

I loved it when he said that.

"Have you seen the checkerboard, Grammy?"

"Next to the sofa, by Poppy's giant jar of cheeseballs," Grammy pointed with her wooden spoon. I hurried through the kitchen and into the living room, careful not to lose my flip-flops.

On dancing day, Poppy dressed up like an old-timey gentleman—brown checkered pants; fancy, black dancing shoes; silky, polka-dotted shirt with his favorite red bowtie; and the dressiest old-man golfing hat he could find to top it off. I threw open the back door and walked out onto the porch, ready for him to swoop me up and start dancing.

But where was he? I stood on the porch and looked around. "Poppy! Oh, Poppppppyyyyyyyy! Where are yoooooouuuuu?" When I headed down the porch steps, I knew something was wrong.

"Grammy!" I screamed. "Grammy! Help!" Poppy lay on his side with dirt all over his face. His eyes were open, but he didn't see me.

I shook him as I tried to get him to look at me. "Poppy. Wake up! It's me. Your Cricketbug."

Grammy scooched in beside me on her knees and checked for a pulse, "He's still alive. I'm gonna call an ambulance."

I'll never forget those sirens as long as I live. As I stood beside Poppy and watched everything, sounds seemed to disappear. All I could see were the flashing lights. The EMT's rolled the stretcher out of the ambulance, at the same time Daddy pulled in. He came up behind me, took my hand, and we sat together on a bench in Grammy's flowerbed. They strapped Poppy onto the stretcher and the driver helped Grammy climb into the back with him. Daddy hugged me as they disappeared around the corner.

I hid my face in his jacket and cried. "Daddy, is Poppy going to be okay?" I wiped my cheek on his sleeve.

"I don't know, sweetheart. I just don't know."

—3—
AT THE HOSPITAL

They took Poppy's pants and made him wear a gown. That's what Grammy called it, but it looked more like a pitiful excuse for a dress if you ask me. Poppy would never wear a dress. If he'd had a choice, he'd have pitched a fit about having to wear that silly little see-through thing that didn't even cover up his hiney. He needed to get up and tell them to give him back his clothes. Then he should tell them not to make grown men wear dresses. That's what he should do.

"Grammy, how long until me and Poppy can play Imagination Checkers again?" I hoped the doctor had given her good news while I was at school.

"It may take some time, Cricket. Poppy isn't responding, and the doctors are still running tests to see what's wrong," Grammy patted the empty seat beside her. "We'll just have to be patient and wait."

I plopped down. "Grammy, do you think it would be okay for me to set up my spare checkerboard in

Poppy's room? You know, in case he wakes up and wants to play."

"I don't see why not, but I'll need to ask the nurses to make sure."

I thought for a minute. "Thanks, Grammy. For now, I'll set it up here on this table and play by myself."

Me and Poppy didn't just play checkers—we played Imagination Checkers. It's where we pretended to be someone else or live in a different time. Before we made a move on the board, we had to do something the made-up person would do. Like the time we were in a zombie apocalypse. I was the only surviving human, and Poppy played a creepy zombie. He kept trying to catch me and turn me into a zombie, but I was too smart for him. I hid behind the bushes and sprayed him with zombie spray. Well, not real zombie spray. It was a can of cinnamon apple air freshener that I borrowed from Grammy's bathroom. Poppy smelled so strong Grammy wouldn't let him in the house until he hosed off in the backyard. At least he was a fresh-smelling zombie.

"Grammy, do you want to play?" Right then, a nurse entered the waiting room and asked for Mrs. Wilson.

Grammy stood, "I'm Lois Wilson. Is everything okay?"

"The doctor will be here soon and wants to talk about your husband's diagnosis. Please follow me," the nurse said. Grammy motioned for Mama to come with her, so I stayed with Daddy at the other end of the waiting room.

"Wanna play checkers with me?" I shook Daddy a little since he was leaned back and sleeping.

"Huh, what? Maybe later, Cricket. We've had a long few days. I'm going to nap a little longer."

So, I played by myself and pretended me and Poppy were fighter pilots in World War II. The moves didn't work without a copilot, so I folded up the checkerboard and set the game by Grammy's crochet bag. I sure hoped Poppy felt better soon.

—4—
KYLE

January 15th
Dear Journal,
   It's official. I'm homebound. No more
school bells. No more recess. No more
friends. Just homebound. They told my
mom I've missed too much school, and
this was the best option. At least I won't
have to repeat fourth grade. A teacher
comes once a week and gives me work
in each subject and then checks behind
me. One of my projects is to keep this
ridiculous journal, so here you go. I'm
basically in isolation just because I'm sick.
It's not like it's my fault, but I'm the
one being punished. Mom keeps telling
me to stay positive. How about this: I am

POSITIVE, this stinks. Is that positive enough for you, Mom?

—5—
MR. NEEDSOME HAS MOVES

Mr. Needsome is my unimaginative fourth grade teacher. Sometimes when he teaches, I feel like I'm going to suffocate and die in my chair because the air I'm breathing is so boring! Poppy says Mr. Needsome "needs some" imagination. I agree. If something isn't a fact, Mr. Needsome won't share it. When he teaches creative writing, roadkill could do a better job. His idea of a creative and fun story is writing about what I want for Christmas.

Today's journal prompt is super boring like always. *Write about one thing you have learned so far this year.* Seriously? Why not something fun like, *Luigi knew he shouldn't take the money ...* or *I opened the door to the tunnel and ...*

When I picked up my pencil to start my boring journal entry, something scurried across the room. I leaned toward Aaron's desk, "Did you see that?"

"What?"

Natalie screamed and jumped up on her desk. Sue and Joni did, too. The girls bounced up and down, waving their arms, screaming and crying. Our classroom was a circus. Fred leapt on his chair and yelled, "The creature ran into Mark's book bag! Look! Over there!"

Everyone turned toward the back corner of the room. Mark twisted around like a slow-motion mime, lifting his feet in the air, away from his backpack.

"Silence!" yelled Mr. Needsome.

The room grew suddenly still. Every gaze focused on the wiggling fabric near the opening of the pack. Mr. Needsome tiptoed to the bookbag and whispered to Mark, "Don't move." Slowly, he lifted the top with the end of his yardstick and a mouse ran out, headed straight for Mr. Needsome's pants leg.

Mr. Needsome danced like he was on the Wii dance board. And, boy, did he have some moves!

"Get it out!" Mr. Needsome yelled as he boogied across the classroom. He was whacking and flopping, desperate to get the mouse out of his pants. Mr. Mouse finally had enough and ran down and over toward the door. Waiting with a small trash can, Mr. Jenson, the janitor, trapped the mouse before he could escape into the hallway. The whole room cheered for our new hero, Mr. Jenson.

Maybe writing my journal entry wouldn't be boring after all.

When we parked, I leaped out of the car. Running all the way to the hospital's glass sliding doors, I urged Daddy, "Hurry, slowpoke. Hurry up! Come on! They won't let me in without you." Daddy finally caught up.

We stopped at the desk in the lobby to sign in and have our temperatures checked. Then I grabbed Daddy's hand and dragged him through the lobby straight to the elevators.

"Poppy's waiting on me. Come on, Daddy." I knew Poppy was ready for a game of Imagination Checkers. "And, boy, do I have a crazy story to tell him about Mr. Needsome and that nutty mouse."

Daddy was patient, even though I wasn't. "If you don't stop pressing the button like a crazy person, you're going to break the elevator, and we won't be able to see Poppy at all."

I put my hands in my pockets and made my best statue impression. Even when the elevator dinged and the doors opened, I didn't break form. Stiff as a board, I waddled to the edge of the elevator and hopped in with both feet, as still as could be. Daddy let me press the button to Poppy's floor. No longer pretending to be a statue, I mashed button twelve. My hand must have slipped because the five lit up too.

Before it shot up, I scooted under Daddy's arm and held on tight. I'm not scared of elevators, but I don't trust them, either. When an elevator stops, it almost throws my belly up to the next floor before bringing my tummy back down again. And this elevator was especially good at belly-throwing. I'm pretty sure before the elevator stopped, my guts were slung straight through to the moon and back!

When the doors opened, there was a boy, same size as me. He was wearing the coolest green bandana with skulls. His hospital gown hung loosely over his red-plaid pajama pants, and he had on purple fuzzy slippers.

"Going down?" he asked.

We shook our heads.

He asked the older lady next to him, "What will it hurt to ride up and then back down? You know I love riding the elevator."

"That's fine. Let's hop on." She reached out and kept the door from closing.

He jumped over the crack and landed right beside me. "I love to ride the elevator."

"Me too," I smiled back.

The doors closed, and my thoughts went back to making sure my belly didn't get thrown too far into outer space. As we shot up to the twelfth floor, I looked over at the boy next to me and wondered why he was in the hospital. He didn't really look sick.

When we came to a stop, I leaned over and said to the boy beside me, "Those are the coolest slippers I've ever seen."

"Thanks!" He smiled.

The elevator dinged, and I was careful to jump over the crack where the elevator met the floor. Grammy told me a story about a little boy who got his shoestrings stuck in one of those cracks. They had to stop the elevators for two hours and get him unstuck. That wasn't going to happen to me.

I waved at the boy as the doors closed and looked at Daddy. "What's wrong with him?"

"Since he is wearing a bandana, my guess would be cancer. Sometimes, the treatment for cancer makes a person's hair fall out in patches or altogether, and they wear a bandana to cover their head up."

"I didn't know kids got cancer."

"Anyone can get cancer, no matter their age."

"Does Poppy have cancer?"

"We don't know anything yet. But I hope not."

I didn't want Poppy to have cancer. For that matter, I didn't want him to have anything. He needed to get better. Just to get better so he could be my Poppy again.

We made the turn at the end of the hall, and I spotted Poppy's waiting room. Grammy and Mama were both crocheting when I barged in. The scene from Mr. Needsome's class popped in my head. "Mama, Grammy, you won't believe what happened today. A mouse got loose in class, made half the kids jump onto their desks, and then ran up Mr. Needsome's pants. He danced around, and the whole room laughed. Then Mr. Jenson captured the mouse under a trashcan, and everyone cheered."

I looked over toward the window outside of Poppy's room. "How is Poppy? Can we play Imagination Checkers today?"

Mama and Grammy looked at each other with one of those grown-up looks.

Grammy said, "Cricket, there's something we need to talk to you about."

—6—
KYLE

January 27th
Dear Journal,
   The doctor moved me to the hospital.
It's not as bad as I thought. I see
other kids on my wing when I'm out for
my walks. I play jokes on the nurses.
Last night, I put a whoopee cushion on
the desk chair. It was hilarious! This
morning, I pretended to be asleep when
the nurse checked my vitals. Just when
she put the blood pressure cuff on my
arm, I popped up and yelled, "Boo!" She
screamed so loudly that everyone ran
to check on her. Ha! Living here isn't
so bad.
   I do miss my friends. Mama said
the doctors think I need to stay here

for a few months until I finish my cancer treatments—four rounds of chemotherapy to be exact. I hate being hooked up to that stupid machine. Ugh. Four months seems like a long time. Mama said she would bring some toys and games by pretty soon. That may speed up the time.

—7—
ROCK 'N' ROLL

When I woke up, all I could think about was playing Imagination Checkers with Poppy. I sprang out of bed, ran to the closet, and dug through my special costume trunk. There I found two clear-plastic candy containers that Poppy and I wore over our heads when we pretended to play checkers on the moon. Poppy thought it would be funny if we stuffed our pants and shirts with newspaper and talked to each other over imaginary radios, just like those people in outer space. Then Grammy wrapped us both in tinfoil. We looked more like aliens than moonwalkers. Poppy looked like he had a little, tiny pea-head compared to all that stuffing in his clothes.

Carefully, I set our space helmets to the side and continued digging. I found our sets of funny teeth that Poppy likes to wear when we don't feel like dressing up all the way. On those days, we put on our Goofy ears and silly teeth. Then, we talk real slow and silly like the cartoon character, Goofy. Poppy laughs just like him, and we giggle until one of us has to excuse ourself to go to the bathroom.

I threw the teeth and ears on the floor, but still hadn't found what I was looking for. On one side of the costume trunk were our tomahawks, baseball jerseys, Mardi Gras beads, and construction worker hats. Knowing that if I could just find the magic costume, Poppy would have to cheer up and feel better, I dug deeper.

At the very bottom, under all the neon-colored scarves and beside a pile of wacky socks, was the magical accessory that would make Poppy's day. I picked up the two pairs of black and neon sunglasses. We got them one night when kids ate free at the Pizza Palace. Reaching way down deep, I finally found the heavy metal rock 'n' roll wigs and fluorescent scarves. Now, I only had to find my inflatable guitars.

While I looked behind the trunk, a knock on the door scared me. "Be there in a sec, Daddy!" I looked all over the closet and still couldn't find the guitars. Imagination Checkers would have to happen without them. We could always play the air guitar, instead.

I shoved my rock 'n' roll outfits in my backpack, slipped on my tennis shoes, and headed for the breakfast table.

Daddy was standing there with arms crossed. "Cricket, you are not going to school in your pajamas. We've talked about this."

Oh no! This time I really did forget.

"Sorry, Daddy." I dropped my bag, ran back to my room, and pulled on a pair of black jeans and a white shirt—it would help my rock star appearance later when we went to see Poppy. Back downstairs, I scarfed my toaster pastry and licked the gooey strawberry filling off my fingers.

"After school, Cricket, I will pick you up, and you will stay at my office until I get off at 5:30. Then we will join your mom and Grammy at the hospital."

Drats. I always had to be so quiet at his office. "Like a church mouse," he always said. What kind of mouse lives in a church anyway? And what in the world was I going to do for two whole hours at his office? I did have my checkerboard, and I could play an imaginary game of Imagination Checkers. It wouldn't be the same without Poppy, but I could practice what moves I would make and how I would act like a rock star.

What if I made Poppy a get-well card? Maybe Daddy's office for two hours wouldn't be so bad after all—if I could just make it through Mr. Needsome's boring class. Maybe another mouse would show up and add some pizzazz to our day. Or what if he was a church-mouse-turned-school-mouse, and I could ask him why church mice had to be so quiet, anyway.

"Cricket, grab your stuff and let's go." Daddy's voice completely derailed my train of thought, and I almost jumped out of my skin! "Did you hear me? Let's go, kiddo."

"Bye, Pedro," I yelled at the tabby cat out front. He didn't look up, just kept cleaning himself. I'm sure glad I don't have to bathe myself with my tongue. I don't even like to lick cake frosting off tinfoil because my tongue always feels so weird. What would it be like to be Pedro and have to lick dirt and grime off my body every night? How in the world would I reach the bottom of my feet? Or my elbows?

When Daddy got in the car, I was trying to see how close my tongue could actually get to my elbow.

"I'm not even going to ask," Daddy said.

"How come cats clean themselves with their tongues?" Daddy always knew the answer to stuff like that.

He sat there just a minute and then replied, "I guess, Cricket, because they can't turn on the faucet or soap up a washcloth."

I hit him on the arm and smiled. "You know what I mean."

"Well? They can't, can they? That'd be pretty funny to watch, wouldn't it? I can see him now. Pedro, standing in the tub, scrubbing his little furry underarms, singing while the water covers his body."

That was a funny thing to picture. Maybe Mr. Needsome's journal would be a free-write this morning, and I could write a story about Pedro the Bathing Cat. Or maybe Pedro the Bathing Cat could show up in another journal. And he could make a daily appearance in every journal this week. What better way to spice up the day than Pedro the Bathing Cat?

—8—
PEDRO

February 23rd
Dear Mr. Needsome's Journal,

One day, Pedro, my super-intelligent and big-brained tabby cat, was on the front steps bathing himself. He was using his tongue, as ordinary cats tend to do. All of a sudden, he started coughing and gagging. All the hair he licked was stuck to his tongue and was going down his throat. He hacked. He did that nasty eyes-popping-out-of-your-head hairball cough and finally, the wad came back up. Pedro hated hairballs. He also didn't like bathing himself with his tongue.

That's when Pedro the Wonder Cat got an idea. Why couldn't he bathe himself like his human friends did? It was revolutionary! He could be the first, the one and only! He could be Pedro the Bathing Cat! He could get a small towel and wrap it around his furry little waist, walk on his back feet, and wear a little kitty shower cap.

I moved my pencil to the bottom of the page and drew a picture of Pedro the Bathing Cat, complete with bathtub and shower cap. While drawing, all I could think about was Poppy in that hospital room.

Did Pedro ever miss his family? He lived with us, his human family, but did he miss his mama, grandma, and grandpa? Could cats even remember their lives before they became a part of a human family? With my crayons, I added the finishing touches to Pedro.

How terrible to be a cat and never know my furry family. How awful to never play Imagination Checkers with Poppy ever again. Or to never know my mama and daddy. I decided that even though Poppy was sick, at least I knew him, so that was way better than the life of a cat.

—9—
KYLE

February 25th
Dear Journal,
    My teacher asked me to write about
what I miss the most. Honestly, I miss
plain, old boogers. I know that's weird,
but I miss the way my old boogers felt
in my nose instead of always having
nosebleeds. I miss my hair, too. I began
my second round of treatments this
week and my hair started coming out
in clumps. Grandma bought me a bunch
of different colored bandanas and I
really like to wear those. It makes me
feel like a motorcycle driver.
    I miss Fridays at the rec center in
my neighborhood. And flag football on
Thursdays during gym class. I miss

my friends at recess and the silly pranks we played on each other. I miss Wednesdays at church with Mrs. Tilley. I miss not being sick. If I could go back in time, I would make it where I never got sick, even if I had to stay on that last well day forever.

At least, I'm on a kid's wing, and there are lots of colors and murals. And I'm really glad my hall doesn't smell like old people. Nana's nursing home smells like old people, and I just can't take the smell.

Mama and Grandma are here a lot. The nurses like me, and I like them. They sneak me lollipops like the bank teller at home. I also have a TV in my room and a DVD player, so they make the time go by faster. Life's not so bad, I just really miss my old life.

—10—
REVEREND SEABURN

By the time we arrived at the hospital, I had my rock star air guitar stance down. It was fun practicing at Daddy's office in the back corner behind his coat rack. Even though all Daddy's permanent markers and pens were black, Poppy's get-well card was a success. On the front, I wrote "etG ellW oonS". Poppy would be able to read the words—it was our own secret, made-up language. On the inside, I drew Pedro the Bathing Cat, our rock star outfits, and a clown holding a bunch of balloons. I knew all the pictures would cheer him up.

The elevator was full of people, so I didn't get to push the button. I held on tight to Daddy as the elevator shot up. Just after my belly fell back into place, I headed toward the opening doors. Daddy grabbed my arm and pulled me back. This was the floor where I met the boy wearing the super-cool bandana and those awesome, fuzzy slippers.

I looked both directions hoping to see him again, but no luck. The mural was all I could see—an ocean complete with dolphins, starfish, clownfish, and kids snorkeling. It looked so beautiful and bright. There was even a giant rainbow at the top with the words "Hope Lives Here."

A lady got off the elevator and stepped in front of the mural. She had a large bag with games inside. I could hardly contain myself as I saw the corner of a checkerboard sticking out.

"Daddy! Daddy!" I whispered. "That lady has a checkerboard in her bag!" He smiled and told me to hold on.

The next stop was the twelfth floor. As the elevator took off again, my poor stomach felt like a slingshot. When we finally stopped, I looked down and the floor was still moving. I jumped over the crack as the doors opened and even when I was on solid ground, I still felt unsteady.

The preacher and his wife from Grammy and Poppy's church got off the elevator with us. He had to be at least a hundred. He walked all stooped-over with a cane and was as wrinkly as one of those crinkled-up Shar Pei dogs like my neighbor used to have. His nose and ears were way too big for his face. And he had false teeth.

Mama and Daddy didn't go to church, but when I stayed the night with Grammy and Poppy on the weekends, they took me to church with them. I tried my hardest not to have to go with them, but most of the time they didn't care that my slingshot needed a new strap, or my Tonka trucks were in the middle of building a road in the big dirt hole. They dressed me up and we drove the ten minutes to Perseverance Baptist Church.

One time, I asked Poppy why the church was called Perseverance. He said a long time ago the church only had a few members. Back then, it was called Corner Street Baptist Church. They didn't even have enough money to pay the light bill, when one of the members asked the Lord what He wanted them to do. He said God spoke out loud so that all seven people heard, "Feed my sheep."

So, every Saturday, they opened the kitchen in the back of the church and cooked a giant pot of soup. They also made sandwiches, and anyone who needed a meal was welcome to come. People heard about the meals and wanted to help. The church started growing, and they decided to change their name to Perseverance Baptist Church. I never understood why they began feeding people instead of starting a farm, but Poppy didn't question it, so neither did I.

On the Sundays I went to church at Perseverance, I sat between Grammy and Poppy. Our pew was toward the front in the very center. Sitting that close to Reverend Seaburn was very hard for me. Most of the time, me and Poppy got in a lot of trouble with Grammy.

See, Reverend Seaburn started preaching, and as he reached the good part of the sermon, he got louder. When his voice got bigger, his false teeth made this clicking sound, almost like Grammy's old typewriter. The pew bounced up and down as Poppy tried to silence his laughter. When I saw Poppy laughing, I laughed, too. It was usually about that time when

Grammy shot us "the look" and we both tried extra hard to quiet the chuckles.

One Sunday, Reverend Seaburn was particularly fired up, and his teeth were popping extra hard. I was looking anywhere but at the stage because laughter was coming at any moment. Off to one side, I noticed something moving on Miss Hilda's walker. She sat right in front of us. Perched on top of her walker, as big as you want to see, was a green money lizard.

Every time Reverend Seaburn waved his arms, the lizard followed, raising his head up and then down. I elbowed Poppy and pointed to the lizard. Just then, Reverend Seaburn pounded his fist on the big, wooden pulpit. That lizard leapt into the air and landed in Miss Hilda's curly, gray hair. Reverend Seaburn must have thought Miss Hilda was receiving a miracle from God because she jumped up and swatted the lizard that was tangled in her hair. The harder she fought, the louder the preaching got. The louder the preaching, the more his teeth popped.

Suddenly, the lizard broke free and jumped onto the stage. Reverend Seaburn, filled with excitement, pounded his fist on the wooden stand once more. The lizard jumped into the fake plant next to the pulpit. Poppy and I held onto the pew just as hard as we were holding our breath. We waited. Waited. Then the lizard made the leap. He jumped onto the pulpit and climbed right up the front. He stopped for a second, looked over his shoulder almost like he was saying, "Watch this!" Then, he climbed right up the skinny microphone and stopped on the puffy end, staring at Reverend Seaburn. The entire room took a giant breath. No one moved. No one breathed.

Reverend Seaburn's teeth stopped clicking. He didn't even flinch—he just stared at that lizard. I felt like I was in a Geico commercial set in a Wild West town—preacher versus lizard in a downtown showdown.

Then he did it. That little lizard jumped onto the enormous nose of Reverend Seaburn. I have never heard a scream like that preacher's.

As he screamed, the lizard ran up into his gray hair and sat there, very still. The preacher froze. He carefully reached on top of his head and tried to snag the lizard. Instead, he grabbed a handful of hair, pulled off his toupee, and launched hair and lizard across the stage! The whole church gasped, and then, we heard laughing. Poppy and I belly laughed until we couldn't breathe. Grammy even laughed, too. Poor old Reverend Seaburn.

So here he was, walking down the hall to Poppy's room right in front of me and Daddy. All I could think about was that lizard perched on top of his head and him ripping his toupee off and flinging it across the stage. I giggled all the way down the hall, and Daddy looked at me like I was crazy.

Oh, how I hoped Poppy was awake when we got to his room. Maybe Reverend Seaburn visiting was a good thing, too. Maybe he could talk real loud, and Poppy would hear those teeth clicking and wake up. Maybe. Just maybe.

—11—
MIRACLE MABEL

Daddy and I stayed a few steps behind the Seaburns after they exited the elevator. "It shows respect letting our elders go first," Daddy whispered in my ear. Who knew I was going to age ten years waiting on them to teeter down that hallway toward Poppy's room? I'm sure glad I didn't have to follow them across a parking lot; I'd be at least a hundred!

Grammy and Mrs. Seaburn were in mid-hug when she spotted me. I was pointing at Reverend Seaburn's toupee and silently giggling. Grammy shot me "the look," so I sneaked to the back of the waiting room and looked into Poppy's room. The blinds were open, and Poppy was sleeping. I picked a chair in the corner and pulled out my rock 'n' roll glasses and wig. If I was going to help Poppy get better, it was time to practice for our game of Imagination Checkers.

When Grammy finished talking with the Seaburns, she turned around and locked eyes with me. "Cricket! You get down from there this instant!"

I was so wrapped up in practicing my air guitar moves, I had climbed up in a chair and was jumping while playing.

"You are going to break your neck one of these days, you and all your silly dance moves!"

I laughed to myself and hopped down, "Grammy, how is Poppy? Is he ever gonna get better?" I took off my neon glasses, rock 'n' roll wig, and plopped down next to Grammy.

"I hope so," Grammy squeezed my hand, "but I don't know for sure. The doctor said he had a stroke, and now he has had a second stroke. This one was very bad, and he may not recover from it. But I am hoping and praying to God for a miracle."

"Like Miracle Mabel?" I asked with excitement.

"Well, not exactly, but something like that."

Poppy used to talk about Miracle Mabel all the time. She was this little girl who grew up in his hometown. Mabel was never able to walk because she was born with a rare bone disease. As the story goes, Mabel sat in a wheelchair and looked out her window every afternoon, watching the neighborhood kids play stickball. Poppy said Mabel had never gone to school, and he doesn't remember her coming outside except to go to church on Sundays.

Then one day, there was a traveling evangelist who came to town. Poppy heard this man could heal any sickness, so he went by Mabel's house to tell her about the man. Mabel's mom answered the door and brought her to speak with Poppy. He said that Mabel looked pale and frail sitting in the wheelchair. He said that as he told her about the evangelist, her eyes twinkled, and he could tell she was excited. She assured Poppy she would be there at seven and would get her long-awaited miracle.

Poppy told everyone in the neighborhood that Mabel was going to be at the service, and the whole town wanted to see if this man was who he claimed to be. The evangelist's tent was packed with people, and many folks stood outside. Poppy said when he got there, Mabel and her mama were already on the very front row, waiting on her miracle. Mabel was wearing a purple dress with a big yellow bow in her hair and a Bible held tightly to her chest.

The evangelist preached. He started soft, and then got louder and louder. He taught about heaven and hell, and how sinners needed to repent before it was too late. Even though the message was important, Poppy said he didn't hear a word the preacher spoke. All he could do was stare at Mabel, who never opened her eyes.

She prayed through the entire service, begging God for her miracle. Finally, the time came when the evangelist called people to the stage to receive their healing. There were two people ahead of Mabel.

The first was an old man who was blind on one side. The evangelist placed his hand over the man's eye, prayed, and his sight was restored. Next was a lady who had extreme stomach pains. He placed his hands on her stomach, prayed, and she said the pain immediately went away.

Next was Mabel. Her mama wheeled her up the ramp onto the stage. Mabel held tightly to her Bible and when she stopped in front of the evangelist, her eyes opened for the first time all night. "Mister. I believe Jesus can make me well. I believe it with all my heart. Will you please pray for me to be able to walk?"

Poppy said you could have heard a pin drop as everyone in the tent held their breath, praying for Mabel to have her miracle.

That evangelist reached out and held her tiny hands, "Sweet, faith-filled, little girl, I don't have to pray for you. Jesus has heard your prayers, and He has already healed you. Get up and walk."

Poppy said there wasn't a dry eye in the place. Mabel lifted herself up out of the wheelchair, stood up for the first time in her life, and walked over to her mother. She held her hands up in the air, praising God.

Miracle Mabel was never in pain again, and she became one of the best stickball players in the entire neighborhood. Poppy said Mabel even ran track when she was in high school. All because she believed God could heal her.

I know Poppy isn't young anymore, and he isn't awake to pray like he usually does, but I sure hope Poppy gets a miracle like Mabel. Even a halfway kind of miracle would be okay with me.

—12—
KYLE

March 9th
Dear Journal,
   I felt pretty good today. I didn't have to keep my IV pole with me, so I sat in the rec room for a little while. There was a cartoon playing and two other kids sat in the room, but they were asleep in wheelchairs. I was hoping someone would come in and want to play a game with me, but no one did, so I worked on a puzzle of the United States.
   I'm halfway through my second round of chemo and then have two more to go after that. I hope I can keep feeling good. Mama says my body is really strong for just being a kid. I still have

my down days, but, overall, it's not terrible.

I've been talking to God a lot more lately. Thanking him for the good days and praying he would make time speed up.

Mama sneaked in Sanford, my chihuahua, yesterday in her purse. It's been two weeks since I held him last. It was so nice snuggling with him under the covers for a little while. Mama took him to Grandma's. She's been looking after him since she lives closer than we do. While he was here, Sanford licked my face until he didn't have any slime left to share! I hugged him a really long time. I wish he could stay. I really need a friend.

—13—
UNRESPONSIVE

"Daddy, Daddy! That's her." I slipped my arm through Daddy's as the doors closed and the mysterious checkerboard lady got in the elevator. I held on tight as my belly flew to the ceiling and quickly landed back in place. Once we stopped on the fifth floor, I watched the lady step out of the elevator and turn right. Maybe she was visiting her son or daughter. Or maybe she was coming to play checkers with someone.

The idea of checkers turned my thoughts to Poppy. Before I left for school that morning, I grabbed our crazy wax lips and silly holographic glasses that make our eyes look really huge. Surely that would cheer Poppy up when I got to see him today.

As we rounded the corner, I noticed Grammy wasn't in the waiting area. I glanced and saw her in the room, sitting beside Poppy. He was lying in the hospital bed, covered with a blanket. His head was turned sideways, and his eyes were closed.

On a table close by were the cards, flowers, and balloons people sent. I guess Grammy found the card I made because there it was in the very front.

I knocked on the glass and waved at Grammy. She looked up, smiled, set down her needlework, and tiptoed into the waiting area. "Toddy's been sleeping all day. Your mom went to get us some snacks and magazines."

"Can I go see him, Grammy? Pleeeeaaaasssseee. Pretty please."

"Cricket, you may come in and talk to him, but Poppy is unresponsive."

"What's that mean?"

"That means when we talk to him or ask him questions, he's unable to answer us."

Poppy couldn't talk. That meant Poppy couldn't play checkers with me. Maybe I could get him to be responsive again. "Can I go talk to him, Grammy?"

"You sure may. I'm just not promising he will even understand you or be able to talk to you. Go ahead and give it a try. I will wait out here for you."

Grammy patted my shoulder as I opened the door and walked toward Poppy's bed. He looked pale and thin, not like the strong, silly Poppy I knew.

I sat down on the edge of the chair and reached out to hold his hand. "Poppy, hey. It's me, your little Cricketbug. I hope they're treating you okay. Even though I told Grammy and Mama you hated it, they're still making you wear that silly dress. At least you can cover up and no one can see your hiney since you're lying down."

I grabbed the card off the table and set it on his chest. "I made you a card yesterday. Yeah, I know it's not very colorful, but I did draw you a picture of Pedro taking a bath. I thought the pictures would make you smile. Oh, speaking of smiles," I reached in my pocket and slipped on my silly glasses. "I brought our wax lips and big-eyed glasses today, hoping you would be up for a game of Imagination Checkers. I've been working all afternoon on some spectacular moves. Do you want to play with me?"

I watched Poppy's face and waited for him to move his lips. "Well, maybe talking isn't very easy right now. Can you just squeeze my hand? One tiny squeeze? For me?" I waited. And waited. And waited. Hoping for a squeeze, a twitch, or even a flutter to let me know he understood. But nothing happened.

My checkerboard was in the next room. Maybe I could set it up and see if that would help. I even thought about putting Poppy's holographic glasses on him to see if that would do the trick.

But deep down, I knew Grammy was right. Poppy was unresponsive, and there was no way I could play checkers when Poppy wasn't really there to enjoy it. I slipped my glasses back into my pocket, stood up, and headed toward the door.

"Bye, Poppy. Hope you feel better really soon. I miss playing with you." As those words came out of my mouth, I could feel my eyes burning. The tears were about to come.

"Daddy, Grammy, I'm going to the bathroom. Be back in a jiffy." Before they could question me, I rounded the corner at a dead run and hid in the ladies' room. I went into a stall and cried until I couldn't breathe. All I could think about was Poppy—my Poppy—lying there. Not able to talk. Unresponsive. Would he ever get better? Would I ever get my Poppy back?

My head fell into my hands, and I whispered through tears. "God, my Poppy believes in you with all his heart. He needs you right now. And I'm asking you to do what you did for Mabel when you made her walk. Do it for my Poppy. I need him. We all need him. I believe you can. So, will you?"

I grabbed some toilet tissue, dried my eyes, and opened the stall. Looking at my face in the mirror, I knew there was no way I could go back to the waiting room with my family. But where could I go?

Immediately, the beautiful mural flashed through my mind. Of course. That would be the perfect place.

—14—
THE FIFTH FLOOR

When the doors opened, I spotted the mural. The ocean scene turned my frown upside down. I made my best fish face and pretended to swim along with the sea life in the painted ocean.

"Hey, what kind of fish are you?"

Embarrassed, I undid my fish face, and threw my hands in my pockets.

"I, uh, I am a, a, a tuna." A tuna? Really? That's all I could think of? I didn't even know what a tuna looked like unless it was in the can.

"Cool. I usually pretend to be an electric eel. The nurses told me crawling on the floor like an eel was too dangerous and germ-infested."

Smiling, I replied, "Hey, didn't I see you on the elevator the other day?"

I looked down at his feet and answered myself, "Of course it's you! No one else in the hospital has such cool, fuzzy slippers!"

The boy grinned, "You like? I have them in seven different colors, one for each day of the week." We both started laughing. "My name is Kyle," he stuck his hand out to shake mine.

"I'm Cricket." We shook hands and I awkwardly put my hands back into my pockets.

"You wouldn't be interested in playing a game with me, would you?" Kyle asked.

A game? Me? Of course, I wanted to play a game. It had been weeks without playing checkers with Poppy. I didn't care if it was a game of gin rummy, I could sure use a little fun. "I'd love to!"

—15—
THIS IS KYLE

"Cricket! Where in the world have you been? We checked all the restrooms, the hallways, the waiting rooms, the lobby, and every nook and cranny we could find! You've nearly worried your grandmother into a heart attack. What were you thinking just wandering off like that?"

"I'm really sorry, Mama. I really am but—"

Kyle rounded the corner behind me and stuck out his hand for my mama to shake, "Hi. I'm Kyle."

Mama stopped talking and stared at Kyle. He was wearing a knee length hospital gown, lime green pajama pants, and a purple bandana around his head. He rested his foot on the wheel of the IV rack that held all his IV bags and tubes, and he was wearing his awesome, purple, fuzzy slippers.

"Kyle, it's very nice to meet you. My name's Anne, and I am guessing you already know my daughter,

Cricket." Mama shook his hand and looked at me with a puzzled face.

Kyle smiled a really huge smile, "Oh yes. We played games all afternoon. She even taught me this great new game called Imagination Checkers. It's the most fun game I've ever played in the whole entire world! We dressed up with these silly glasses and funny looking wax lips. Every time one of us took a turn, we did something silly with our props. I don't know who won the actual checkers game because the other part was so much fun, and I told her I wanted her to come back every day and play with me. If that's okay with you, Mrs. Anne."

Mama looked at me and gave me a tiny grin. "I think we can work something out, Kyle."

A thought suddenly ran through my mind. "Hey, Kyle. Didn't your mama want you back by six-thirty?"

"Oh man, you're right! I gotta go. Thanks for playing with me, Cricket. See you later, Tuna Fish."

"It's a deal, Electric Eel!" We both giggled as Mama looked at me with a puzzled smile.

When Kyle left, I told Mama all about seeing the lady on the elevator who had a checkerboard, her getting off on the fifth floor, and how beautiful the mural looked. I told her about Kyle sneaking up on me while I was pretending to be a fish and going back to the rec room to dig through the bag of games his mom brought. Once I saw the checkerboard, I had to teach him how to play Imagination Checkers, because I knew he would absolutely love it.

After we got done talking, I walked over to the window to look in on Poppy. Mama said he was still unresponsive and most likely would stay that way for a long time. Poppy would love to meet Kyle. Maybe when he feels better, we can teach one more person how to play, and have teams of Imagination Checkers. That would be so much fun.

If Poppy ever feels better.

—16—
PILLOW FIGHT

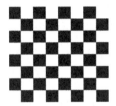

"So, what did you decide?"

Kyle smiled really big, "Today we are going to be boxers, but instead of real boxing gloves, we are going to use these feather pillows."

"Ohhh, I like it!" I said as I imagined the two of us whopping each other after every move. "I'll set the board up in the rec room. You sneak the pillows down here."

I watched Kyle wave to the nurses at the station and walk back into his room. He wore his blue, fuzzy slippers today with his matching blue, skull-and-crossbones bandana. Kyle had the best sense of style I had ever seen.

He looked over his shoulder as he sneaked out of his room with a pillow under each arm. We smiled at each other and thought the coast was clear. Out of nowhere, one of the nurses headed him off.

"Pillows need to stay in the rooms, Kyle," the nurse said.

Kyle shined a sweet smile at the nurse. "I know. But today is a special occasion. I have a new friend who came to see me, and I have permission to unhook from my IV pole for an hour. We thought we could sit on the floor in the rec room while we play checkers today."

The nurse thought for a moment, "Okay, just for today. But make sure you put those pillowcases directly in the laundry hamper afterwards."

"Thank you! And I will," Kyle said as he walked into the rec room.

"That was some fast thinking," I told him.

Kyle handed me my pillow. "Tell me about it. I almost stuttered and gave our plan away. You know, we better set up on the far end of the room, so they can't see us from the nurse's station."

I agreed, and we moved the checkerboard down to the last table.

Before long, the game was in full motion; hits from the side, whacks from the top, the run-jump-pounce combo, undercut swats, and full body smashes. Poppy and I had never had a boxing day, so this was all brand new.

Out of nowhere, Kyle caught me by surprise when it wasn't his move and knocked me in the side of the head. He was gonna pay for that! Trying to get a free pillow whack, we chased each other around the rec room. We knocked over chairs, tripped over toy cars, flipped over the checkerboard sending all the pieces flying. One piece shot in the air and launched across the room as the blades of the ceiling fan caught it at just the right time. We giggled and chased each other some more.

Kyle caught me, pinned me in the corner, and whacked me so hard the pillow busted. Feathers went everywhere. While he was distracted by the feathers, I got one last, good wallop and my pillow busted too. Even more feathers went everywhere.

We grabbed feathers, held each other down, and stuffed them down each other's shirt. Boy were they itchy! A voice jolted us back into reality.

"Ahem," the voice said, loud and gruff. Frozen, we locked eyes with the nurse Kyle had talked to in the hall. "This doesn't look like lounging and playing checkers, Kyle."

"Well, you see, I uh," Kyle began.

"What I see," the nurse paused and smiled, "is two kids having a bit too much fun."

We both blushed.

"It was fun," Kyle said.

I looked his way. "It sure was."

The nurse smiled again and leaned over to whisper, "Let's make sure to clean up all that fun before your mom gets here in a few minutes, Kyle. Here are a couple of trash bags. And hurry."

Both of us let out a deep breath and fell backward on the big bean bag. "Whew. I'm not sure who won that one, but I am definitely a fan of boxing day!"

Kyle nodded as we leaned forward and grabbed the two garbage bags. "For real!"

We shoved all the feathers into the bags and hid them behind the door to the rec room.

"Same time tomorrow?" I asked.

"You bet!" Kyle exclaimed.

We said our goodbyes at the elevator. As the doors closed, I spotted a rainbow fish on the mural. Poppy always said rainbows meant good things were coming. Being friends with Kyle was definitely a good thing. I just hoped the rainbow meant that Poppy would get better too.

—17—
NINJA ACTION

"Got the belts! So, what's this big plan of yours?"

"Ta-dah!" Kyle lifted two small, round laundry baskets and two bandanas. "Take a guess."

"Cowboy bandits?"

"Nope."

"Chicken thieves?"

"Wrong again."

"I give. What are we gonna do?"

"Teenage Mutant Ninja Turtles! Leonardo and Donatello to be exact." Kyle dangled the two bandanas in front of me.

"I'm Donny!" I grabbed the purple bandana. Carefully, I wiggled through his room with the laundry basket, trying not to knock over anything. A belt hooked through the holes perfectly and then I wrapped it around my body. The basket stayed humped on my back just like a turtle. I helped Kyle get strapped in and we tied bandanas around our foreheads.

Kyle reached under his bed and gave me the handle of an old broom. "Now, for the final touch. Here is your weapon."

"Where did you get this? And how come the nurses don't know?"

"Right place, right time," he smiled.

I slid the broom handle down my back, through the belt and basket, and somehow managed to make it hold still.

Kyle reached back under his bed and came out with a plastic pirate sword. "Well, it's not perfect, but it will do." We both laughed and peeked out the door.

The coast was clear. Kyle went first and gave me the signal. Since he had to bring his IV pole with him, he had to be extra careful. We tiptoed through the waiting area, past the elevator, and down to the rec room.

I heard a few snickers behind me, so I knew the nurses saw us sneaking down the hall. They were used to us by now. Kyle already had the checkerboard set up, so we got right into Imagination Checkers.

After some great spin kicks, twists, and forward thrusts, we called it quits for the day and took off our laundry basket shells.

"You win, and I'm beat." He collapsed onto the giant beanbag in the corner, careful not to upset his IV pole.

I plopped down right beside him. "Poppy met a real ninja one time."

Kyle's eyes brightened as I continued. "He was deployed in Japan after the war. He and a couple friends had a day off. They were walking through the market area in town when he saw a fast-moving, shadowy figure out of the corner of his eye. He grabbed his buddies, and they followed the figure. After about a half hour, his two friends gave up and headed back to base, but Poppy continued on, certain he could find the mystery person.

"Suddenly, a hand reached out of the shadows and covered Poppy's mouth. The hidden person pulled him into a room that had only a dim candle in it. 'Soldier,' the ninja whispered in hard-to-understand English, 'do not be frighten. We here protect American soldier. All time you here, we protect.' After he said this, the hidden person backed away and blew out the candle. Poppy said he vanished as if he never existed in the first place.

"When Poppy found his way back into the streets, his friends were waiting for him. He told them the story, and none of them believed him. No matter what Poppy said, his friends were never convinced. But Poppy knew the ninjas were there, and he never forgot what happened.

"For the whole three years he was stationed in Japan, he remembered catching movement in the shadows. He was convinced the whispers he heard in the night were actually those special, friendly ninjas watching out for him and his fellow soldiers.

"The crazy thing is they never had any trouble while they were over there. And I know why. It was the ninjas."

"Man. How cool is that! To actually meet a real ninja? Your Poppy is one lucky dude." Kyle said as he seemed to drift off to some other place in his mind.

We both jumped when we heard a knock on the open rec room door, "Kyle, I'm off work early today."

"Hey, Mom," Kyle said.

She sat down at the table beside us and looked our direction. "And you must be Cricket."

"Yes, you're right," I smiled as I jumped up to shake her hand.

"And you're the lady I saw in the elevator with the bag of games."

Kyle's mom smiled and nodded.

"And, I am also the mom who says it's time to clean up and get ready for supper," she said with a smile.

"It was very nice to meet you," I said.

"You too, Cricket. I'm very glad Kyle has a new friend."

I waved at Kyle and made my way toward the elevator. Tomorrow was my day to choose our Imagination Checkers game. It needed to be a good one.

—18—
DO NOT DISTURB

Drats. The lobby was empty. I hoped to see someone sitting in a chair. Then I wanted to sneak up behind them and breathe loudly in their ear.

There was one little old lady in the corner, but I decided not to scare her. She would probably faint, and I wouldn't be able to dress up for Imagination Checkers anymore. Maybe I would try to scare Kyle during our game, instead.

We made it to the elevator, and I held on tight. Daddy said that before I saw Kyle, I had to check in with Mama and Grammy.

I leaped off the elevator and sneaked down the hall to Poppy's waiting area. The nurses snickered as I passed, which made me smile behind my plastic mask.

Grammy spotted me and let out a shriek, "What in the world is this foolishness coming around the corner?"

She laughed and gave me a big hug.

"Grammy, how's Poppy?" I asked as I lifted my mask.

"About the same, sweetheart. He's not responding. They are feeding him intravenously. That means they have a tube hooked to his body and the food goes inside of him through the tube. He's too weak and unaware to eat on his own." Grammy looked toward the window to Poppy's room. "They don't know how long he will be this way, Cricket."

I missed Poppy. I missed the way he smiled and laughed. I missed his jokes and goofy voices. I even missed his silly snore when he fell asleep in the recliner after eating too many cheeseballs. But I especially missed Imagination Checkers with him. At least Kyle knew how to play, and I could get in a few games with him while I waited on Poppy to get better.

I hugged Grammy and told her I was going to play with my new friend, Kyle, for a little while. Mama piped up from somewhere around the corner, "Be back by six. We have to get home in time to do laundry for tomorrow."

Lowering my mask again, I breathed deeply and loudly, just like Darth Vader, "Yes," breathed some more, "ma'am." Then I ran toward the elevator.

Grabbing the handrail inside the empty elevator, I took a deep breath, and pressed number five on the keypad. Maybe it was because the elevator was almost empty, but it hardly threw my belly at all. I was pretty happy about that.

When the doors opened with a ding, I smiled under the mask. There was the amazing mural of the ocean. I stood and looked at the fish for just a minute and then headed to Kyle's room. As I rounded the corner, I saw that something wasn't right. The blinds were rolled down in Kyle's windows and the light was turned off. His door was closed and there was a sign on the outside that read, "Do Not Disturb."

I was just about to knock on the door when someone came up behind me and whispered in my ear. "Kyle's not feeling very well today."

The voice was unfamiliar, and I turned around to see an older lady about my grandma's age. "My name is Ruth. I'm Kyle's grandma." She smiled as she stuck out her hand to shake mine. "Let me guess, you must be Kyle's new friend, Cricket."

"Yes!" I lifted my mask and smiled. "So, you've heard of me?"

"Oh yes! He's told everybody who comes by about his new friend. And if they sit down long enough, he teaches them how to play Imagination Checkers. As a matter of fact, he sent me to the store to pick out silly outfits and big belts. Yesterday evening, we dressed up like exterminators. The day before, we wore red pillowcases on our shoulders and pretended to be superheroes. I haven't laughed so hard in a really long time." Ms. Ruth smiled and then said, "Let me guess, you were planning to be Darth Vader and Luke Sky Walker today."

I pulled my mask back down and did my best Darth Vader breathing impression. "Yes, you are right." I took off my backpack and pulled out the light saber and Luke Sky Walker outfit. "I brought this for Kyle." I looked down at my feet for a second, "but if he's not feeling up to it, I guess I will have to wait until next time."

"Well, Cricket. I know I'm just a grandma, but I actually know a thing or two about light sabers."

My eyes looked up and met hers. "Oh, yeah?"

"Yes. And I really like that Luke Skywalker fellow."

"Ms. Ruth, are you saying you want to play Imagination Checkers with me?"

"That's exactly what I'm saying."

I thought for a minute. "Well, I guess that'd be better than nothing."

We pulled a chair in front of us, got situated in our costumes, and let the game begin. Every time she attacked me with her light saber, I countered with mine. Back and forth we went until I had her checker pieces trapped. Or so I thought.

"Double jump. Read 'em and weep, kid."

My jaw dropped. "How? What? I didn't even see that move."

"Well, maybe I learned a few tricks from Kyle over the last couple days."

Smiling, I took my mask off and sat down beside Ms. Ruth. There was a mural on the wall directly ahead of us. It was a wizard dressed in a blue robe, wearing a pointed, cone-shaped hat on his head. He had a wand which he waved and sparkly colors shot out of the end in all directions. There were cute, fluffy forest animals sitting around watching like they were in a happy trance. Underneath the scene were the words "Mysteries, Wonders, and Miracles."

All I could think about was the wizard in an old cartoon I used to watch. He could do anything with his magic, including making an empty costume come to life and dance around the room. If he was sitting in this waiting area, he could wave his wand and bring the fish mural to life, too. And he could take that Do Not Disturb sign off Kyle's door and we could play Imagination Checkers.

"I sure wish wizards were real," I said out loud.

Ms. Ruth smiled. "I imagine they could do some neat stuff with those wands. But you know what, Cricket? God is powerful, too. And his power is real. We just have to have faith."

Faith. I sure could use some of that right now. "Well, I don't care if it's a wizard or God or something else, I just want Kyle and Poppy to feel better real soon."

"Me too, Cricket."

THE HOSPITAL FROG HOP

March 25th
Dear Journal,
   That last dose of chemo was terrible.
I puked all night long. Grandma said
Cricket came by to play. I hope she
comes back soon. We had so much fun
playing Imagination Checkers the other
day. Before I got sick, I already taught
three nurses, Grandma, and Mama
how to play. Watching Grandma run
around with a cape pretending to be
Superman was so funny.
   You know, up until this week, I was
pretty sure God wasn't listening to
me anymore. I thought my prayers to
have a friend were bouncing off the

ceiling. But then he sent Cricket, and she taught me how to play Imagination Checkers. Now everything is fun again, even though I still have cancer. I'm so thankful for my new friend.

March 25th
Dear Mr. Needsome's Journal,
   Finally, we have a free-write. Instead of more Pedro stories, I will tell you about my new friend Kyle. He is nine years old, just like me. He loves games, especially Imagination Checkers. He's silly and fun to be around.
   But Kyle's sick, which sometimes makes it hard to play with him. There are days when he can't have any friends around. Sometimes he gets weak and has to rest. But other times, he is loud and rambunctious, just like me! The nurses always come in and check on him when we are in the middle of one of our silly games. They watch and laugh.
   Kyle is the best friend I've ever had except my Poppy. I sure wish Poppy would wake up so they could meet each other. The three of us could have so much fun.

"Cricket," Kyle mouthed, "Hurry! Come on," he motioned with his hands. Kyle grabbed my shirt sleeve and pulled me into the room, then slammed the door and shut the blinds.

"What have you got? Why are you whispering?"

"Ta-dah!" Kyle handed me a shoebox. "Open it. No. Wait. Let me." Kyle carefully cracked open the lid. Inside were two of the biggest bullfrogs I'd ever seen. "I found them this morning in the fountain when I was out for my walk. What do you think?"

"What do I think?!? I think they are just about the coolest things I've seen all day! But how in the world did you get them into your room?" I asked.

Kyle leaned in and whispered, "I convinced Grandma Ruth to get me a bottle of cold water out of the soda machine down by the fountain. Since I already had my box with me collecting pebbles to throw into the water, I grabbed the frogs while her back was to me and held the lid down tight. She never even noticed."

"Boy, you're sneaky."

Kyle smiled slyly. "Do you want to let them out and see which one will jump the farthest?"

"You mean like our very own frog hop? Oh, man. Yes. Let's do it!"

I peeked around the corner, made sure all the nurses were occupied, and motioned for Kyle to stick the tape down onto the waiting room floor. It was the perfect place for a race.

My frog was the dark-colored one and I named him Spike. Kyle decided to call his Jeremiah, like the old song my Poppy used to sing. I never understood why

71

the guy was drinking wine with a bullfrog, but I loved to hear Poppy sing that silly old song with his deep, gravelly, bullfrog voice.

We both hurried back to Kyle's room, our hearts beating in our throats. Kyle grabbed the box and I checked around the corner one more time. The coast was clear. I reached into the box, grabbed Spike with both hands, and held him down at the starting line. Kyle pulled Jeremiah out of the box and held him down next to Spike.

At the same time, we whispered, "On your mark, get set, GO!" We let our frogs go, ready for the excitement of our first hospital frog hop.

But they just sat there. We poked them. We whispered little froggy words of encouragement. We quietly cheered them on. Neither one of them moved. Just when we were about to give up, the elevator dinged. It was like they had been waiting on the starting bell.

Jeremiah and Spike immediately took off. A little old lady stepped off the elevator just as the frogs were heading her way. We both knew what was happening, but there was nothing we could do to stop what was coming. She set down her heavy purse at the exact moment that Jeremiah leaped into the air, and he landed right inside her handbag.

I half-smiled at the little, old lady, grabbed Spike, and ran to the room. Kyle beat me there and was peeping through the blinds to see which way the lady went.

"What are we going to do?" he asked.

"I don't know, but we better act fast." I grabbed the shoebox. "You get your IV pole and let's go for a walk. That way we can follow her. I will act like I'm carrying a gift for someone in the box. You distract her and I will reach into her purse and rescue Jeremiah."

"Okay, let's do it."

We followed the lady all over the children's wing until she finally stopped at the nurse's station. "Could you help me?" She plopped her purse up on the counter.

Kyle and I stopped breathing as the lady kept talking.

"I have the room number written on an envelope in here somewhere but I just—"

And that's when it happened. Jeremiah leaped out of the purse, straight into the woman's face. With the grace of a bear, the woman lost her balance and fell backwards onto the floor. As she was going down, the lady reached out, hoping to grab something that would brace her fall. The only thing she could grab was a fake shrub in a plastic pot. As the plant fell on top of the little old lady, Jeremiah lunged into the air, legs extended behind him in perfect ballerina form.

When everything got still, Jeremiah was sitting in the middle of the lady's face, the shrub was across her belly, and her purse was turned upside down on the floor next to her. The three nurses hurried around to help her up, and one of them reached for Jeremiah. Just as she cupped her hands to capture him, he jumped straight into the air and into the pocket of the second nurse's scrubs.

"Get it off," she screamed, "Get it off, now!" Another nurse reached out toward her co-worker's pocket and tried to seize the runaway frog.

Just then, Jeremiah decided he didn't like the pocket anymore, and made one giant leap. He slipped right through her hands and landed in the hair of the third nurse. She looked like she was riding a hundred miles on a bicycle in five seconds as her legs pumped up and down and her hands waved around. I think she tried to scream but instead, her mouth was frozen in place, as wide as it would open. We laughed until our faces hurt.

Kyle grabbed Jeremiah and became the instant hero of the fifth floor, complete with applause, hugs, and cheers from all the nurses. I cracked the box open on the other end for Kyle to slip Jeremiah back inside.

"Spike is missing," Kyle whispered through smiling, gritted teeth.

We both looked up just in time to see Spike sitting on the edge of the cafeteria cart beside the desk.

"Uhh, we, uhh, we, um better get going," Kyle stuttered as we backed away from the nurse's station. We waved to the nurses and wore fake smiles until we got around the corner and out of sight.

As we made our way down the hall, back to Kyle's room, we heard a huge ruckus and dinner plates crashing to the floor. "I think they found Spike," I whispered. Both of us smiled and laughed.

We decided to head downstairs and put Jeremiah back in his natural habitat. We made sure to get permission from a nurse who walked with us back to the fountain. Once we got outside, Kyle reached into the box, pulled Jeremiah out, and released him at the edge of the fountain. As we watched Jeremiah disappear into the water, we held hands, used our best bullfrog voices, and sang Poppy's favorite old song.

—20—
THE SECRET STAIRS

"Kyle, did you hear what happened to Spike?" I asked as I ran around the corner into his room.

Kyle shook his head.

"I overheard some nurses on the elevator who said they opened the door to the back stairway for the frog that got loose on the fifth floor."

"That's great news," said Kyle.

"No, it's not great news. Did you even hear me? Spike might still be in the back stairway. What if he's trapped? We need to make sure he gets out," I exclaimed.

"Oh, wow. You're right. I bet he's hungry."

"Do you know where the back stairs are?" I asked Kyle.

"Maybe. I know there is a back elevator where they send the laundry and where food is sent on rolling carts. Wherever there is an elevator, there is usually a set of stairs." Kyle paused and thought for a minute, "Do you remember where Spike got loose? I think it's down that back hallway, but we are going to have to be very sneaky to find out. Let me grab my IV pole and we can go for a walk around the fifth floor."

We headed out of the waiting area, toward the rec room. Instead of entering, we took the hallway to the right. I waved at a few of the younger kids and Kyle spoke to some of the older ones. We took another right, and then another one. Next stop was the nurse's desk where Jeremiah had put on his show.

"Why, hello, Kyle. It's nice seeing you out for a walk today."

"You, too, Nurse Sarah," Kyle quickly replied.

"And is this your new friend who plays checkers with you?" the nurse asked.

"Yes, this is the one. Nurse Sarah, meet Cricket," Kyle said.

I waved and smiled.

"It's nice to meet you, Cricket. Kyle has told all of us nurses about the fun you two have together." My face turned a little red and so did Kyle's.

Thankfully Kyle was quick on his feet, "Hey, Nurse Sarah. Maybe you can help me with something. I've been giving Cricket a tour of the fifth floor, and she asked me how we get laundry and food up and down from the first floor. I know there is a place somewhere on this wing where the laundry is sent and where the food magically appears. Would you mind giving us a quick tour?"

She looked over her shoulder, leaned forward, and whispered, "Technically, I'm not supposed to show you, but if you promise to keep it a secret, I can walk with you there."

We both nodded and followed behind Nurse Sarah. *Hang on, Spike. We are coming for you!* I wanted to shout, but I kept my words to myself. As we reached the end of the hallway, we both took a deep breath and waited for Nurse Sarah to speak.

"This is the staircase that leads to the first floor. We use this stairway only in case of emergencies." She pointed to the left, "And here is the elevator that you were asking about. We only use it to transport meals and laundry."

"Oh, cool," I said, remembering to play along. "I always wondered how they got stuff up and down from all the floors in the hospital without anyone seeing them do it. Having an elevator in the back makes tons of sense. Thanks for the tour, Nurse Sarah."

"You two are very welcome. Now, get to your room before anyone knows you were back here."

We nodded and made our way back to Kyle's room. If Spike was still in that stairwell, we needed to plan a rescue. And fast.

—21—
OPERATION RESCUE SPIKE

"Okay, so I've spied all morning. The nurses have a pattern. Right after meals, and also after mid-morning snacks, the food ladies gather all the plates and put them on carts. Once they have their carts full, they fill up the elevator and take everything downstairs. When they head down, the nurses start their rounds. They begin on the other side of the fifth floor, where the really sick kids stay. Did you know those kids aren't allowed visitors unless each new person is sanitized first? I'm glad I'm just a little sick and can still have regular visitors.

"Anyway, afternoon snacks just happened. They are picking up plates right now, and my room is usually the last room. Are you ready to go?"

"Oh, yeah. Operation Rescue Spike, here we come!"

As soon as the lunch lady left Kyle's room, we walked into the waiting area. We pretended to look at the giant fish mural, but headed for the stairs when we saw the last nurse leave the hallway. "Kyle," I whispered, "did you remember the cardboard to prop the doors open?" We sure didn't want to get locked out and trapped down there.

"Yeah, got it right here," he held up the pieces, then slid them back into his pocket.

We tiptoed across the hallway in front of the nurses' station and ducked under the countertop. Once we got to the other end, we checked behind, in front, and to our sides. The coast was clear. Leaving his IV pole behind a cluster of fake trees and bushes, Kyle went first, and I followed. Kyle placed the cardboard in the crack of the door.

"Whew. We made it!" Kyle whispered as we stepped onto the first stair. "Now, to find Spike."

We walked down the first flight of stairs. Every now and then one of us would whisper, "Spike." The second flight of stairs showed no signs of a frog and neither did the third. Once we reached the fourth set of stairs, we both saw something move toward the bottom. We hurried down and there on the last step was Spike.

"Spike!" We whisper-shouted.

Kyle picked him up and carefully set him in the box. We smiled and made our way down the last flight of stairs. Without thinking, we pushed open the door and rounded the corner to set Spike free. As we spotted the fountain, Kyle and I looked at each other and froze.

"We forgot to put the cardboard in the door," I said quietly.

"We are locked out," replied Kyle.

"What are we gonna do?"

"Let's get to the fountain. We will think of something." Kyle was trying to stay positive.

We sneaked through a construction zone and made it to the fountain. Sitting on the edge of the concrete was Jeremiah. "It's like he was waiting on us."

I picked him up, gave him a hug, and then we set our frogs beside each other on the ledge. As if on cue, Spike and Jeremiah jumped into the fountain and went for a swim.

"You think Jeremiah was waiting on Spike?" I asked.

"Sure seemed that way," Kyle replied, as he sat down beside me on the bench.

"Now, to the next problem. How are we gonna get back inside?" I asked.

—22—
NOW WHAT?

We walked around and around the fountain for a bit, trying to come up with a plan. We even walked back to the door. It wouldn't budge.

"Maybe we can go back around to the front entrance," I offered.

"We both know that won't work. We didn't get permission and we will be in big trouble. Only kids with grown-ups can get in that way, but maybe we could walk around to the other side and hope there is a door that was left open somewhere."

"I don't know, Kyle. You know how strict they are about locking things up around here." We walked over to the entrance of the stairs and shook the handle one more time. The door was still locked.

"Hey, Kyle, isn't that employee parking over there?" As we scanned the parking lot, we saw Nurse Sarah heading to her car for her break. Ducking, we hoped she didn't see us. "That was a close one," I whispered.

"Wait a minute," Kyle thought out loud. "Maybe Nurse Sarah could get us back in."

Before I had time to stop him, Kyle began yelling, "Hey, Nurse Sarah!"

I could see the panicked look on her face as she got closer and realized we were outside by ourselves. "What in the world are you two doing out here? You aren't supposed to be outside unless you're with an adult."

Before I could stop myself, I started talking a mile a minute. "Do you remember when the frog got loose on the fifth floor? Well, that was our frog. We were actually having a frog hop, but he jumped into that lady's purse. We had another one named Jeremiah, but we caught him. Spike is the one that got away. Then I was in the elevator and heard one of the nurses talking about how she let the frog out down the back emergency steps by the laundry elevator, and I just knew we had to check on him and make sure he got reunited with Jeremiah in the fountain.

"So, we tricked you into showing us the back elevator and back steps and then we sneaked out and forgot to leave the door wedged open, and by the time we realized our mistake, it was too late, and the door had already closed behind us. And now we are stuck outside. But, oh, we did find Spike, and he was on the next to last flight of stairs, and we delivered him to his home in the fountain, and Jeremiah was there waiting on him.

"We are sorry we tricked you and we won't ever do it again. So, can you please, pretty, pretty please help us get back inside?"

Nurse Sarah sighed deeply and thought for a minute. "Well, now. That is quite the story. And how do I know you will never pull this kind of shenanigan again?"

"Because of the pinky promise," Kyle quickly jumped in. "The pinky promise is the deepest promise a kid can make, and kids will do everything within their power to never break it. We pinky promise we will never, ever trick you or try to sneak out of the hospital building ever again." Then both of us stuck our pinkies out in front of us.

Nurse Sarah thought hard and finally agreed. She linked her pinky with each of ours and then said, "I'll go in and get a wheelchair, so others will think I'm taking you and your friend out for a walk. I'll be right back."

Kyle and I let out all the breath we had been holding. "That was some quick thinking, Kyle. I think you saved us," I said as I elbowed him in the side.

"Yep. Since Nurse Sarah helped us before, I hoped she would help us again," Kyle said, as he sat down on a bench. "And Spike is safe now and living with his best friend again. I'm so glad we found him."

"Me, too. This whole frog hop thing got way bigger than I ever imagined."

"But, boy, was it fun!"

We both nodded and laughed.

"Okay, you two." Nurse Sarah rounded the corner with a wheelchair. "I'm back. Kyle, hop in and let me sneak you two back inside." We laughed some more and went back in with Nurse Sarah.

—23—
ONE-EYED WALLY

April 15th

Dear Mr. Needsome's Journal,

Kyle told me he has a type of cancer called leukemia. I think I want to research it for a project in class. Sometimes, it's like Kyle doesn't have anything wrong at all, and then other times, he can't even get out of bed. I thought maybe he was homeschooled, but he said he is homebound. That means he has a teacher who checks on him once a week and gives him assignments to complete. He is moving to my school next year once he finishes his treatment. Maybe he will be in my class. Oh, we would have so much fun together. I can't wait until next year!

"Oh no! Kyle, I have to go. It's almost six!" Army day had been one of our best games ever. We pretended to be soldiers during WWII crawling through the trenches, dodging bullets, and using code names.

Poppy used to tell me stories about when he was in the war. He said that one night they were hiding in a bunker, and the rain was pouring down. The enemy's lights were circling, daring one of the American soldiers to step into the beam. All of a sudden, the rain started to hurt. It wasn't rain, it was hail.

They huddled under jackets and burlap sacks, desperate to protect their bodies from the painful stings. Then, without any warning, the light went out. All the American soldiers could hear the commotion in the enemy's camp, and they knew this was the distraction they needed. They grabbed their weapons and charged. Poppy told me if that hail hadn't broken the light they would have surely been killed.

I told Kyle all of Poppy's old war stories, and then, we acted them out. We had so much fun. Too bad we had to quit. As I waved goodbye to Kyle, I walked into the open hallway that connected to the waiting room.

My heart sank to the floor. There in the waiting room, just outside of Kyle's room, was the meanest, scariest, longest-armed, old man that had ever walked the face of the earth. And he was just sitting there like he belonged.

I plastered myself against the windowed wall and tried my best to become a chameleon. What if he saw me? What if his arms got to me before I could get back into Kyle's room? My mind was reeling with questions and fear. Slowly, I slid my back against the wall and scooted around the corner into Kyle's room.

I let out a deep breath and stared at Kyle, unable to even speak.

"What's wrong, Cricket? You look like you just saw a ghost."

I motioned for Kyle to come close, and I shut the door. We peeked out the window of his room. "It's One-Eyed Wally," I whispered. "He's here."

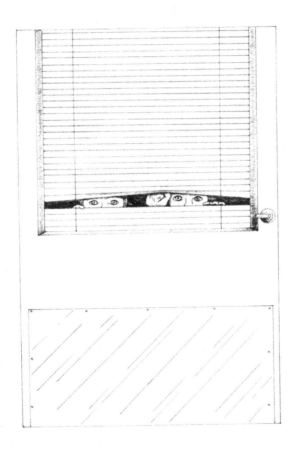

—24—
WALLY WABANOSE

"When Poppy was a teenager, there was an old, abandoned house at the end of his road. At night they saw lights flickering even though no one lived there. Sometimes they could hear moaning from the upstairs window. And other times, they could hear an evil laugh coming from the porch as the rocking chairs rocked on their own.

"Then one day, someone moved into the house. He was an old man who walked with a cane. He never smiled, and he yelled at anyone who came close to his house. But the strangest thing was he always wore a patch over his right eye.

"Poppy and his friends tried to imagine what happened to his eye. One of his friends guessed he was born that way. Another said he was in a fight, and someone shot him. Another one said his eye was ripped out by a shark while he was on the open waters as a pirate. After lots of discussion and research, they finally agreed this wasn't your ordinary old man. This was, in fact, the long, lost pirate, Wally Wabanose. He had come back from the sea to protect his treasure that was hidden in the basement of the old, rickety house.

"Poppy and his friends used to dare each other to sneak into Wally's house and see if they could find the gold. No one wanted to be called a yellow-bellied sap sucker, so they all took turns. Two of his buddies made it in and out with no problem, so Smitty, Poppy's best friend, decided to give it a try. He sneaked around back and was going to slip in through the basement window. It was dark, so he shined his flashlight into the basement's eerie blackness.

"Sheer terror overcame him! He couldn't even scream, the sight was so awful. His beam of light was shining directly in the face of One-Eyed Wally!

"The angry old man reached his ten-feet-long arms through the empty window and grabbed Smitty's collar. 'Get out of my house!' Then the gravelly voice got louder, 'If you ever come back, I'll kill you with my bare hands!'

"Smitty dropped his light and ran. He said he'd never seen arms reach that far or hold on that tight in his entire life. Ever since then, nobody dared mess with One-Eyed Wally."

Kyle and I sat there on the floor thinking about how scared Poppy and his friends must've been. We both hugged our knees until Kyle finally broke the silence, "I've got an idea." He sneaked over to the window and peeped through the blinds to see if Wally was still there.

Immediately, Kyle switched back into Army mode, "Soldier Cricket, I have a mission for you, should you choose to accept it."

I jumped to my feet and stood at attention. "Sir! Yes, sir! What is my mission?"

"Soldier. There is a row of empty chairs that will act as a barricade. At all times, keep those chairs to your left. You will have to belly crawl all the way to the elevator exit so that no one will become wise to your presence. Once you make your way to the other side, I will slide your backpack across the floor, and you will be home free."

"What about you, General Kyle?"

"I will hold down the fort until he leaves. I will be safe here. You are the one who must survive."

"Okay, let's do it!"

Kyle and I ducked inside his room and shut off the lights. In the dark, he smeared lines of camouflage paint on my cheeks. I adjusted my fatigues and pulled my lid down tight.

Kyle peeped around the corner. "He's looking the other way; now's your chance. Go, Cricket. GO!"

I squatted down beside the door and slowly pulled it open. Quickly, I hit the floor in a full-on belly crawl. Out of the corner of my eye, I saw Wally shift his body and knew I had to move even faster. Three chairs. Two chairs. One chair. Ahhhh. I made it!

From my new hiding place behind a giant potted plant, I took a closer look at the man in the waiting area. The guy was definitely One-Eyed Wally. He had the patch, cane, and creepiness all wrapped up in one.

I looked back at the dark room and motioned. "Kyle," I mouthed and held up my hand. "Kyle!" But there was no movement in his room. I waved and signaled some more, but it was as if Kyle had disappeared.

—25—
POPPY'S AWAKE

April 20th
Dear Mr. Needsome's Journal,
   Kyle's gone. Wally ate him. He must
have reached into the room with his ten-
feet-arms while I was crawling behind
the chairs. No one will ever believe me,
but I know it was One-Eyed Wally. I
wish Poppy was awake because he would
believe me. And he would know exactly
what to do. Maybe I'm wrong. Maybe
it's not too late for Kyle. Maybe Wally
hasn't finished him off. I can hope. Oh,
what am I going to do?

I looked everywhere for a sign of struggle—searched the lobby for drag marks, the café for anything out of place, and even checked the bathrooms. Opening my trench coat, I pulled out my notebook.

No sign of struggle on 1st floor.

Quickly, I slipped the book into the hidden pocket of my coat. Kyle's only hope was me, and I had to do everything I could to find him before Wally finished him off.

As we boarded the elevator, Daddy made me put away my magnifying glass. "People are starting to stare," he whispered in my ear. I didn't even care.

The door opened to the fifth floor and Daddy pulled me back, "Don't even think about it. Poppy first, friends second." Once we landed on the twelfth floor, I pulled out my notebook.

No sign of foul play on elevators. Will check for prints later.

Grammy met me at the door to the waiting room. "Poppy's awake."

I totally forgot about Kyle as I rounded the corner and almost knocked Poppy's door down trying to get to him.

"Poppy!" I shouted and sat down in the chair beside his bed. Poppy turned his head toward me and opened his eyes. He had a look that seemed to stare straight through me. It was like he was there but, then again, he wasn't.

Even though I knew he probably wouldn't understand, I started talking anyway. "Poppy, you won't believe everything that has happened since you got sick. A mouse ran up Mr. Needsome's pants and then he came out. Mr. Jenson caught him with a flipped over trashcan.

"Then one day here at the hospital, I accidentally ended up on the fifth floor, and I was pretending to be a fish, and this boy named Kyle started talking to me. He wanted to play a game, so I taught him Imagination Checkers. We have been playing every day since, and we've been boxers and Ninja Turtles, and we played with the googly eyes. It's been so much fun, and Kyle is just the coolest, and now that he knows how to play, we need to get another person to learn how to play and we can have teams in Imagination Checkers and ..."

Poppy closed his eyes and rolled back over like I wasn't even talking.

I reached out and held his hand, "And when you get to feeling better, we're gonna have so much fun. You have to feel better, Poppy. You just have to."

A tear rolled down my cheek as I held Poppy's hand, "I love you, Poppy," I whispered as I set his hand down on the bed.

I walked out and smiled at the thought of Poppy getting better, but I was also sad that he didn't understand me. "Baby steps, Poppy," I whispered to myself. "You will get there."

—26—
WE KILLED THE GOATS

I sat in the waiting room making my list of possible places to search for clues about Kyle's disappearance, when a hand suddenly gripped my shoulder.

"You scared me to death!" I yelled at Grammy. She was trying to get my attention, but nearly scared the pooey out of me, instead.

"Oh, sweet girl. I'm sorry. I just wanted to say hello." She patted me on my head and went to sit with Poppy a little while.

That moment of being startled made me think about the time that Poppy and I were playing Imagination Checkers and were dressed up like ghosts. Neither one of us knew what we wanted to dress up as, so we went into Grammy's sewing room and found two old sheets. Poppy grinned as he cut eye holes in the middle of both sheets. "She'll never even know they're gone," Poppy whispered and smiled. We pulled the sheets over our heads, grabbed some rope to tie around our waists, and headed to the porch for some Imagination Checkers.

Before each move we made, we did something a ghost would do. We made spooky noises and waved our arms around. Then Poppy got the wild idea to try and scare his old cat, Oscar.

There Oscar sat— by the neighbor's fence. We sneaked down the steps and hid behind an old pecan tree. "On the count of three," Poppy whispered, "let's jump out from behind the tree and run towards Oscar."

I nodded and smiled.

"One, two, three!"

"Ahhhhhh!" we screamed as we ran toward the old, striped tomcat. Oscar barely even flinched, and he definitely didn't run. But something terrible happened.

IMAGINATION CHECKERS

We killed our neighbor's goats. All twenty of them completely fell over deader than dead right there in the pasture beside the fence. Poppy yelled and whooped trying to get their attention, but none of them moved. We threw pebbles, hoping to scare them, but nothing worked. Poppy even slipped through the fence and poked one of them, but it was useless. They were dead. And it was all our fault.

We slid our ghost costumes off and sadly dragged the sheets to the porch. We told Grammy everything, and she was horrified.

"Well, what's done is done," she said. "Let's give those goats until the morning, and then, you two need to call the neighbors and tell them how sorry you are for booing where you ought not be booing." Grammy was right, and we knew we were done for.

First thing next morning, Poppy called me, "Cricketbug! You're never gonna believe this. It's a miracle! All the goats are alive. I guess either me or you did some serious praying last night, because every single goat is awake ... and grazing in that pasture."

I couldn't believe my ears. Quickly, I slid on my slippers and ran next door to Poppy's in my pajamas to see this grand miracle with my own eyes.

About the time I got there, our neighbor walked up, "These goats are about the strangest critters I've ever run across. I fired up my lawn mower last week, and they passed out for two hours. Then last night, something must have spooked them again because they passed out just the same. I guess the man who gave them to me wasn't kidding when he said they were called fainting goats."

Poppy and I looked at each other with a smirk and just laughed. Ever since that day, if one of us gets spooked or scared, then the other one falls out on the floor and pretends to be one of those fainting goats. I almost fell on the floor after Grammy scared me, but I don't think she would have appreciated it as much as Poppy.

"Oh, Cricket," Grammy said, "I almost forgot. One of the nurses left this for you. She said to check your small, zippered pocket on the front."

—27—
HE'S ALIVE!

My backpack! That meant Kyle was okay. I grabbed the bag and sprinted to the other side of the waiting room. In the zipper pocket was an envelope with a note inside.

Dear Cricket,
Kyle asked me to write you this note because he knew you would be worried that One-Eyed Wally had finished him off. I have no idea what he's talking about, but he said you would understand. He said to tell you he made it out alive.
The reason he didn't give you your backpack was because he passed out. He's on a treatment for leukemia, and it can affect his blood sugar levels in an unpredictable manner. The nurses took good care of him, though, and he

is better now, You may not get to play many games with Kyle over the next two weeks, but he said he would still like for you to come by, His treatment is very hard on his body right now, and he will be resting a lot, Thank you, Cricket, for being my son's friend, You have helped bring so much sunshine into his life during this difficult time,

See You Soon,
Ms, Rena

Kyle was alive! What a relief. I took off my detective coat and slipped it into my backpack. I checked with Grammy and headed up to see Kyle. Maybe he would feel like company for a few minutes.

As I made my way through the waiting room on the fifth floor, I could see Kyle's face beaming from his room. I ran in there and gave him a big hug. "I really thought you were a goner. I was sure Wally had eaten you."

"I knew you would think that. But he didn't. That's why I knew I needed my mom to write you a note and get your backpack upstairs to your grandma." Kyle said. "Oh, by the way. Can you keep a secret?"

—28—
CHANGES ARE COMING

April 24th

Dear Mr. Needsome's Journal,

   I am overriding your boring topic today and making it a free-wrwite instead. I just can't concentrate. I know I should be happy for Kyle, I really should. I mean, he has lived for nearly three months in a hospital, and now he might get to go home. He is so excited. But I just can't get excited. His home is too far away for us to see each other, and there is no way to play Imagination Checkers over the phone. Kyle is my best friend. He can't leave.

April 24th

Dear Journal,

Can you believe it? The doctor said after this last round of treatment, I will be free to go home! I miss my house so much and my old school and all my friends. Well, not all my friends. My best friend is Cricket, and she still has to live here. That's the only sad part about going back home. I won't get to hang out with her and play games all the time. Maybe I can still come visit, or maybe she can come to my house. I don't know how it is going to work, but I do know I have to come up with a really good game of Imagination Checkers to play before I leave the hospital.

—29—
KING KYLE AND QUEEN CRICKET

"Tooooot, toooot, toooot! Hear ye, hear ye! Please welcome QUEEN CRICKET!"

Two nurses met me as I got off the elevator, and they draped a deep purple robe around my shoulders. Then another nurse placed a paper restaurant crown on my head. Finally, Kyle's grandma placed a jeweled scepter in my hand.

She bowed and whispered, "His lordship, King Kyle, is awaiting your arrival."

My breath caught a little as I took my first step onto the red carpet. No one had ever gone to this much trouble for a game of Imagination Checkers before.

The waiting room was plastered wall-to-wall with paper painted like castle bricks. Just outside of Kyle's room were two giant thrones facing each other. Between them was a small table with a checkerboard on it. It was like a scene I could only imagine in my dreams. And there was Kyle, standing beside his throne, scepter in hand, robe and crown in place. He was waiting on me to join him for the most perfect game of Imagination Checkers anyone had ever played.

Slowly, I princess-walked down the red carpet. I drew my fingers together into the best queen wave I could and smiled and waved to the invisible crowd that was waiting on my arrival. I could see children clapping, mothers and fathers cheering. I nodded in their direction, smiled, and continued toward the throne.

As I reached my seat, King Kyle nodded, "Welcome, my lady. Shall we begin?"

"We shall, indeed." I replied.

Kyle made the first move. He summoned a guard, "Bring me the thief who stole from our castle." One of the nurses brought a child from down the hall. "Thief, what do you have to say for yourself?"

"I am innocent, your lordship."

"Queen Cricket, what shall we do with this lying thief?"

I stood up and pointed my scepter at the thief. "OFF WITH HIS HEAD!" The guard escorted the thief away. Kyle and I both giggled. "I've always wanted to say that."

My turn to move was next. "Guards, bring me the man who stole macaroni from the king's table." One of the nurses brought another child up to our thrones. "What say ye, macaroni thief?"

"What say, who?" he asked.

"Enough, peasant. Effective immediately, you will receive forty lashes with a wet spaghetti noodle." Kyle and I giggled again and then regained our composure.

It was Kyle's move. "Guards, bring us the lady who is the keeper of the scepters." One of the nurses slowly led Kyle's grandmother to the foot of his throne. "Woman, many jewels are missing from my scepter as of late. What have you to say?"

"O lordship, 'twas my dog. He eats everything, including children's homework." Kyle's grandma slyly bowed as we silently giggled. "Please, have mercy on an old woman and her dog. I am sure the jewels will come out in a few days, just like the coins he swallowed last week."

With that, the entire group that had gathered on the fifth floor fell out laughing. Kyle's grandma smiled but never broke form.

Once the laughter died down, Kyle stood and pointed his scepter at his grandmother, "For your honesty, I will spare your life. Follow your dog all day and all night. When he poops, bag it, tag it, and report your findings to the head guard. You are dismissed!"

"Thank you, O King. Thank you, my Queen. I shall not forget your immense kindness. Never shall I neglect the breath in my lungs." She continued thanking us for sparing her life as she backed away from the throne. Kyle and I just giggled.

After several more moves and many more shenanigans, Kyle jumped my last checker and shouted, "ROYAL CHEF! Bring us our supper!" Two nurses bowed and disappeared down the hallway. They quickly returned with two giant-sized chocolate sundaes loaded with sprinkles and covered in hot fudge.

"Your supper, my lordships," one of the nurses said, as she set our ice cream on the table in front of us.

"You thought of everything, Kyle!"

Kyle smiled and took a bite of his ice cream. A nurse came close and whispered something in his ear, and he smiled a giant smile. "Hurry and finish your ice cream, Cricket. I have one more surprise."

As we sat on our thrones eating, talking, and laughing, I heard the elevator ding. All the nurses hurried over to the door, like ants moving a crumb. They were obviously hiding something.

Kyle stood up and held his paper towel roll trumpet to his mouth, "Tooot, tooooot, tooooot! Hear ye, hear ye! Please welcome his lordship, SIR POPPY!"

—30—
SIR POPPY

There he was. My Poppy! Awake. Weak. But trying to smile. Two nurses placed a bath robe over his shoulders and around the back of the wheelchair. Another nurse gave him a fly swatter for a scepter and set a plastic colander on his head for a crown. Grammy, Mama, and Daddy stood behind him, all smiling and crying.

Grammy spoke, "When we saw he was awake, we knew he wouldn't want to miss this for the world!"

I threw down my scepter, flung my robe and crown aside, ran down the red carpet, and gorilla-hugged my Poppy. Tears ran down my face as I hugged him and didn't let go. Finally, I felt someone tap me on the shoulder. I turned to see Kyle standing there.

"Well, aren't you going to introduce me?"

I smiled, laughed, and cried all at the same time. "Poppy, this is my best friend, Kyle. Kyle, this is my Poppy."

Kyle bent down on one knee, gently grasped Poppy's limp hand, and shook it. "Your reputation precedes you, Sir Poppy. The pleasure is all mine."

Kyle smiled and then quickly stood back upright. He leaned over and whispered something in Grammy's ear. She smiled and nodded.

I stood up, too, wiping my eyes, and Kyle and I made our way back to the thrones. A nurse put my robe and crown back on and another handed me my scepter.

Grammy pushed Poppy to the front of the red carpet, facing the thrones.

Kyle walked toward Poppy and began, "Today, in the presence of all these witnesses, I have the privilege to introduce the man who started it all. Queen Cricket and I would be lost without your great discovery, oh kind man. You have added joy to a sad boy's life, and life to a sad boy's friend." Kyle grabbed his scepter, lifted it straight into the air, and gently placed the end on Poppy's shoulder. "And so, my lordship, we knight thee, Sir Poppy of Imagination Checkers Land! All hail, Sir Poppy!"

"All hail, Sir Poppy. All hail, Sir Poppy. All hail, Sir Poppy." The room of friends, family, and nurses cheered and chanted again and again.

I stood next to King Kyle, held my scepter up in the air, and touched Poppy's other shoulder. "To you, Sir Poppy, I give all of my love, forever and ever and ever."

A whispered noise slipped from the motionless lips of Poppy, "I love you, too, my Cricketbug."

My heart melted and the tears fell. Poppy was back. God actually heard and answered my prayers. It wasn't a Mabel kind of miracle, but it was a miracle, nonetheless.

This was the best day ever.

—31—
LAST DAY OF SCHOOL

"Cricket, you have to get out of bed. You are going to be late for your last day of school."

I could hear Daddy's voice, but I was playing Imagination Checkers with Kyle and Poppy. The three of us were chefs in a fancy restaurant. Poppy got the crazy idea to start a flour fight, and we were running around chasing each other. Kyle dumped a cup of flour on my head just as I threw a fistful of flour at Poppy's belly. We were laughing hysterically when Poppy got a crazy idea. He laid down on the floor in a pile of flour and made flour angels. Kyle and I were laughing so hard our stomachs were hurting.

"Just what in the world is so funny, young lady?"

This time I jumped out of bed. "Oh my gosh, Daddy. I am so sorry. I was dreaming that Poppy was making snow angels in a big kitchen, but we didn't have snow, it was flour that we had been throwing at each other and ..."

"And I really want to hear your dream—just tell me in the car. We have to go, like NOW!"

I pulled on a pair of jeans, grabbed my backpack, ran down the stairs, kissed Mama and Grammy on the cheek, and said, "Give Poppy my love. Tell him I will come by after school." They both nodded. I snagged my granola bar and juice off the counter and headed for the car.

As we rounded the corner of our driveway, I saw a moving truck pull in next door. Grammy sold their house and moved in with us since Poppy would never be able to live at home again. I'm not real happy with them selling the house, but I kinda understand why. Grammy found a really nice nursing home that is only five blocks away. It's great because I can hop on my bike and ride over there in the afternoons now.

Poppy's body is almost completely paralyzed from his strokes. Grammy said paralyzed means he can't use certain parts of his body anymore. But he tries hard to talk, and we can understand him most of the time. The physical therapist said he might be able to move his hands again, but it will take a lot of therapy. Maybe one day, he will be able to hold a checker again. I can hope.

Kyle will be moving soon, too, but he didn't say where he was going. I sure hope it's closer than where he lives now. Maybe we can get together over summer break since there won't be school.

"So, Cricket, you are mighty quiet this morning." Daddy totally derailed my whole train of thought, "What's on your mind?"

"Just thinking about Poppy and Kyle and that moving truck at Grammy's."

"There's a lot to think about lately. A lot of change."

"Daddy, do you think Pedro knows what's going on? I mean do you think he picks up on all the changes?"

"Well, I don't know, Cricket. I have noticed he stays around the house a lot more lately. And have you noticed he sits with Grammy a lot? I think maybe he knows she's a little lonelier than she used to be."

I smiled as I thought of Pedro sitting in my Grammy's lap. Then I laughed out loud as I imagined Grammy and Pedro, both in bathrobes and shower caps, standing in front of the mirror, brushing their teeth together.

Before Daddy could ask what I was laughing at, I shouted, "Daddy, guess what?" Daddy jerked the car. "Today is my last day of fourth grade. Today is my last day in Mr. Needsome's boring class. Tomorrow I will be a fifth grader!!! WOOHOO!!"

Daddy smiled and pulled up to the curb. "Don't forget, we are going over to meet our new neighbors tonight after you get back from Poppy's, so don't stay too long." I nodded and waved as I skipped to class.

—32—
THE NEW NEIGHBORS

May 25th

Dear Mr. Needsome's Journal,

I have not been very fair to you, Journal. You have helped me a lot this year. Even when the topics were boring, it has been fun writing to you every day. If nothing else, it was enjoyable letting Pedro the Bathing Cat make appearances on Mars, on the bus, in a restaurant, at a job interview, and on a roller coaster. Oh, and don't forget when Pedro got to teach for the day. He taught us the trick for getting those hard-to-reach itchy places! I'm not a big fan of using my teeth, though, so I will just stick to using my hands.

So, today is the last day of fourth grade. Goodbye, Mr. Needsome's Journal. May you rest in ... piece. Get it? Like piece of paper? Haha. Okay. Bye for now.

When I got home, I hopped on my bike and rode over to Poppy's. He was up in his wheelchair, but his body was all slouched down. After setting a baseball cap on his head backwards, I hung a thick gold chain around his neck. We definitely looked like rappers. Even though Poppy couldn't really do much, I wheeled his chair over to the checkerboard. He tried to smile and whisper a few words here and there. I made moves for both of us and tried to be as silly as possible, for Poppy's sake. I even made up a rap that I sang as we played.

"Yo, yo. It's your turn to go. Make a move, make it smooth. Yo, yo. It's your turn to king me. But just 'cause I'm winning, don't mean you can ping me."

Even though he couldn't smile with his mouth, I knew Poppy thought my rap was funny because he was smiling with his eyes. After we finished our game, I had the nurse take our picture. There was something about hanging all these silly pictures on the bulletin board that I thought would help Poppy get well faster.

As I wheeled Poppy back to his bed, I got down on my knees and held his limp hand in mine. Looking deep in his eyes, I whispered, "I love you, Poppy."

Poppy tried to lift his head and whispered, "I love you, too, Cricketbug."

And then I felt it. A squeeze. Not a very big one, but a squeeze. I held his hand tighter, squeezed back, and told him, "Always."

As I pedaled home, I had a smile on my face that wouldn't wipe away. Poppy squeezed my hand! Mama and Grammy wouldn't believe this.

"But Mama, I don't want to meet our neighbors. Today was the last day of Old Boring Needsome's class, Poppy squeezed my hand, and Kyle and I are supposed to talk on the phone tonight. It's been a really good day and meeting our new neighbors who are moving into my Poppy's old house would just make for a bad night."

"It's good manners. Now stop your bellyaching and let's go."

I saw the liftgate to the moving truck propped on the porch. Men were going in and out carrying boxes and furniture. As we got closer, I noticed there was a bike, about the size of mine, leaned against the side of the house. Then I saw a box of Tonka trucks that looked just like the trucks I had in the dirt hole out back. As we walked around to the front of the house, I heard a voice coming from inside.

"But Mom, I don't want to meet our new neighbors. Tell them to go away. I'd rather just move in with Grandma Ruth."

As Daddy put his hand up to knock, our new neighbors pulled the door open. Everyone froze. At first, no one could utter a word, then the endless hugs and greetings happened.

"What are you doing here?"

"No, what are you doing here?"

"You mean ... you bought ... you moved ... you are my new neighbor?"

Kyle and I hugged and talked at the same time, then we ran toward his new room in his new house, which just so happened to be next door to mine.

COMING SOON!

CRICKET AND KYLE: THE SECRET DOOR

The Secret Door begins with Cricket and Kyle plotting to build a catapult in Kyle's bedroom. When the heavy book falls to the floor, there is a hollow THUD. After rearranging furniture, they discover a secret door to a hidden room under Kyle's bedroom.

Cricket and Kyle seek the help of Crazy Crookens, the kooky old librarian who drives a fire-engine-red convertible and knows everything there is to know about Orange Prairie. She shows them a map of the Underground Railroad, takes them on a wild ride, and gives them a history lesson they won't soon forget. Packed with humor, history, and adventure, this sequel is sure to keep all fans of Cricket and Kyle reading and wanting more.

ABOUT THE AUTHOR

Christy Bass Adams, M.Ed., is a used-to-be elementary school teacher who has a fondness for bad jokes, boogers, and bugs. As a boy mom of two, she has become an expert on trains, tractors, Transformers and trucks. She has a "flashlight under the sheets" love for literature, which she shares with her children, who love to stay up late reading great books.

When Christy was a kid, if she wasn't reading or organizing her baseball cards, she was found with a baseball in hand, on the basketball court, or in the top of a tree. Her imagination, much like Cricket's, took her to worlds that no one else visited.

The love Christy has for creative writing began in fourth grade under the instruction of her all-time favorite teacher, Mr. Harvey Waldrep. Sadly, there was a season as an adult, that Christy gave up on her writing dream for over a decade, convinced it was pointless. But God knew she needed the proper encouragement and opened door after door for her to step through. Now, recognizing how important dreams are, she regularly hides in her secret world, only accessible with pen and paper, allowing her imagination to come to life.

Adulthood is overrated and Christy refuses to become an old, fuddy-duddy. Often called silly, goofy, or weird, she gladly wears those labels and encourages others to join her in the creative pursuit of joy. Life is too short to be confined to the shell of a frown.

Currently Christy's day job is the Outreach and Connections Coordinator at Fellowship Baptist Church where she keeps the church family connected with each other and to the needs of the community. Christy, her husband, and their two silly boys find their home at the end of a dirt road in North Florida where the fish are always biting, and the firepit is forever welcoming. She would love to have all her readers follow her at her blog, www.christybassadams.com, and stay up to date with all her new adventures.

MEET THE ILLUSTRATOR

Lisa Isadora Thompson received her BA from University of South Florida in 2001 and her MFA from Florida State University in 2004. Since 2005, she has taught a wide variety of art courses at North Florida College in Madison, FL, where she is also the curator and director of the Hardee Center for the Arts.

In her most recent drawings and paintings, Thompson illustrates the magic of life and seemingly infinite possibilities through the lens of childhood using her own children as subjects. Additional projects have included private commissions. She is excited to be embarking on this new adventure illustrating children's books.

EXTRA! EXTRA!

LETTER TO MY READERS

Dear Readers,

First of all, thank you for reading my debut novel, *Cricket and Kyle: Imagination Checkers*. I hope you have fallen in love with the characters as much as I have. They have been my companions for the last ten years and I'm pleased to introduce them to the world.

I began writing this story when my oldest son was a baby. Every night I pulled our beanbag into the bathroom while Carter splashed in the tub and wrote scene after scene. The story has been finished now for three years, but I let fear keep me from sending the book to publishers. Finally, the need to share this story with others grew bigger than my fear and I took a chance. You are holding, in your hands, a dream come true.

If I were sitting across from you right now, I would tell you several things. First, never give up on your dreams. Whatever gift or talent God has given you, offer it to him and use it well. Never hide it or downplay your abilities; we need what you bring to this world.

The same is true for your unique personality; always be yourself and stand up for what you believe.

Make friends with people who don't look and act like you. Sit with the kid who has no friends. Try every new thing you can. And be okay with rejection and failure—but never let it define you.

Let your imagination run wild. Write, draw, build, create, dance, play, and soar. Never let a day go by where you don't have fun and laugh.

For those who are curious, no, Poppy is not based on a real character, but his silly spirit exists in my parents, grandparents, and myself. Laughter and imagination play a big part in my family. As for Cricket, she is like me at that age in many ways, but her imagination is bigger than mine ever was. She is also brave, bold, and outgoing where I was shy. Our taste in clothes and toys, though, is spot on. And yes, Cricket is my favorite character.

When I was teaching elementary school, I had a student in my class who was diagnosed with Leukemia and transferred into a homebound setting for schooling. Eventually he had to stay a few months in the hospital, but was back in school the next year, healthy and ready to learn. Kyle's character was loosely based on this situation. His personality is uniquely his as I didn't have any friends exactly like him when I was younger.

Cricket and Kyle faced hard situations, but in the end, they were able to come out on the others side smiling and laughing. Never forget, we need each other, just like Cricket and Kyle showed us in the book. No matter what sickness, hardship, or situation comes your way, with God, family, and friends there is light on the other side. Always keep your faith.

Always stoke your joy. And never, ever get too old to have fun.

Always Up to Something,
Christy Bass Adams

AUTHOR VISITS

Christy wants to come to your homeschool group or school. Thanks to advances in technology, Christy can visit in person or via online meeting platforms. Please check out her website, www.christybassadams.com, and request a visit today.

TEACHERS AND PARENTS

Do you want to dig further into the topics and themes discussed in this book? Christy has classroom connections and a discussion guide available for free on her website. Just hit the subscribe button and you will receive information on how to access these free items. www.christybassadams.com

IMAGINATION CHECKERS STARTER KIT

Are you interested in playing Imagination Checkers with your friends and family? Visit Christy's shop on her website, www.christybassadams.com, and order your own Imagination Checkers checkerboard, along with a set of costumes for your first Imagination Checkers game.

JOIN CHRISTY ONLINE AND JOIN THE MOVEMENT!

Christy would love to see you, your family, and friends playing Imagination Checkers. Share your action pictures with Christy using the hashtag: #imaginationcheckers.

Follow Christy and PLEASE send pictures:
Facebook: Christy Bass Adams
Instagram: christybassadams
Pinterest: christyadams88
Twitter: christyadams008

DID YOU LIKE MY BOOK?

Write a review! One of the most helpful signs of support readers can offer to their favorite author is to write a review on Amazon, Goodreads, or other book buying site. Another helpful piece is visiting their website and subscribing to their mailing list. Authors LOVE to stay connected with their readers and this is a great way to get firsthand knowledge about future books and new directions. Thank you for supporting this book!